Thirsty Are The Damned
A True Vampire Anthology

Edited by Charlotte Emma Gledson
and Lyle Perez-Tinics

Rainstorm Press
PO BOX 391038
Anza, Ca 92539
www.RainstormPress.com

ISBN 10 – 1-937758-07-9
ISBN 13 – 978-1-937758-07-3

Library of Congress Control Number: 2011960525

Thirsty Are The Damned: A True Vampire Anthology

Rainstorm Press http://www.RainstormPress.com
Copyright © 2011 by Rainstorm Press
All rights reserved

Interior book design by –
The Mad Formatter
www.TheMadFormatter.com

Cover Design by David Naughton-Shires
www.TheImageDesigns.com
Vampire Picture: sambriggs.deviantart.com
Vampire Model: courtneyrose666stock.deviantart.com

Table of Contents

The Unholy Bride of Julian Tyrell
Joe Filippone

Even locked away in his large master bedroom, the laughter and gaiety from the party was still loud; seeping through the heavy wooden door. Eden still couldn't believe she was at an actual party in The Hollywood Hills. Some of the biggest names in entertainment were there and she, a small town girl from Idaho, had actually talked to them. It felt like a dream. A spectacular dream she hoped she would never awaken from.

The heavy curtains had been opened and the only light came from the full moon. It's pale lavender blue light illuminated them like a spotlight on the lead actors. It had begun to rain and the soft droplets gently pitter-pattered against the window creating a romantic feeling.

Eden also couldn't believe that at that very moment she was alone and naked with Julian Tyrell. She had never done anything like this. She had just met the man that afternoon and here she was with his head buried between her legs, moaning wantonly as he stimulated her.

She just couldn't help it. There was something magnetic about Julian. He was suave, debonair, tall, dark and incredibly handsome. A living, breathing replica of the men in the romance novels she devoured. It was his accent; some kind of East European that she couldn't place, that had really done it for her. Men with accents were her biggest weakness.

With one hand Eden grasped his large brass bed for support as his tongue rapidly flicked against her wetness. Her other hand tightly gripped his soft, thick hair; an unnatural inky black color. Her legs wobbled and he clutched her hips roughly, keeping her in place. Biting her lips she moaned. While she didn't have that much experience with men, she could safely say that Julian was, hands down, the best.

"You taste so good," he gasped looking up at her, eyes sparkling with lustful hunger; accent making her grow even wetter.

"Don't stop," she begged forcing his head back down between her.

Giving her firm bottom a playful smack he continued his oral pleasure.

Eden's stomach tightened. Her heart raced and she closed her eyes tight. She was so close. Just as she was about to take the plunge her eyes snapped opened and she screamed as Julian drove his fangs into her moist, sensitive flesh. His grip tightened, trapping her as he sucked the blood from her body.

As the hot liquid trickled down her legs, Eden's eyes rolled back in her head. Her legs trembled and she began to sweat as her heart rate slowed. Growing dizzy, she felt the room rock back and forth. It reminded her of the time her father had taken her sailing and she had gotten sick.

After Julian had drunk his fill he slowly rose, kissing her stomach; leaving a little bloody trail along her body.

Standing before her, he lovingly caressed her chin. He kissed her and she felt her blood seep between her now dry, chapped lips. Eden felt like she was floating as the sticky metallic liquid slid down her throat.

"You will be my new bride," Julian whispered licking the excess blood from her lips before planting a delicate kiss on them. "Would you like that?" He asked moving a wisp of hair away from her face. "My beautiful Garden of Eden?"

"Yes," she whispered in a far away voice as her eyes, glassy, stared straight ahead.

Smiling, Julian leaned in and sucked her neck, preparing her creamy skin for the final act which would make her his for eternity and seal her fate. A small gasp spilled over her lips as his fangs once again broke through her delicate skin. Holding onto her shoulders he didn't stop until he had drunk every last drop of blood in her body.

Eden, skin a sickly gray-yellow hue and stretched tight across her bones, fell into him with a dusty moan. Carefully Julian laid her in his bed and made love to her. After he had ejaculated inside her corpse-like body he covered her with his great-great-great grandmother's quilt.

"Rest my dear. The transformation is the worst part." Kissing her cold, sweaty forehead he returned to the party before his guests grew suspicious.

Looking back at her, he smiled bitter sweetly. He had so many brides tucked away in his mansion. They were all young girls who had come to Hollywood with stars in their eyes. Like Eden they had all been innocent. Naïve. So trusting. Too trusting. It had been almost insultingly easy to lure them to his mansion. All he had had to do was mention all The Hollywood Royalty that would be present at his lavish parties and they were his. Forever.

Closing the door he left the young girl, shivering and moaning with the coldness of death, to complete her transformation in private.

* * *

Slowly Eden's eyes opened and a bolt of white hot pain shot through her eyeball, penetrating her brain. She was dizzy and her body ached. There was a strange tingling radiating throughout her and her stomach growled painfully. It felt like she hadn't eaten in years.

Getting to her feet she walked over to the full length sparkling mirror; completely lined in gold.

When she saw the monster staring back at her, she let out a shrill primal cry that rattled the mirror's sensitive antiquated glass.

What had he done to her?

Her skin was a macabre gray. Her eyes were sunken and an

unnatural yellow. The wounds on her neck where he had bitten her were pink, puffy and crusted with dry black blood. Julian's bloody kisses were tattooed on her belly and breasts. A dried river of blood ran down her legs and she threw up when her eyes fell on her mangled, torn vagina. It looked like a rabid dog had chewed it to shreds. The most shocking change was the large razor sharp fangs that now filled her mouth. Her lips had recessed back to accommodate them and her gums were still bloody from when they had broken through. The pointy fangs glistened and dripped with acidic green venom.

Crying out she fell to her knees as hunger pains brutally assaulted her. Her eyes welled out and she desperately clawed at her stomach hoping to relieve the pains.

I need to eat, she though desperately moaning out.

Weakly she pulled herself up and, with an animalistic growl, went in search of food.

* * *

"Julian..." Bernadette's silky voice caressed his ear.

"I told you never to disturb me when I'm with one of my brides." He responded annoyed, not bothering to look at the old woman who had been with Julian's family for generations.

The old witch's long, skeletal fingers lazily clenched and unclenched the red paneled door frame. Through the sheer bed curtains she could see Eve's form beneath him. She was his favorite. A silent film star, she had been Julian's first bride. In an ironic touch he had ripped out her vocal cords so she would always be his silent film star. Eve's neck still bore a large hole which she kept concealed with a large scarf. Unless she was in Julian's bed.

"I'm sorry to disturb you Julian," she said. "But your newest bride has gone out in search of food."

"So let her eat if she's hungry," he answered voice rising,

10

desperate to get back to his carnal activities.

"Do you think that's wise?" She asked. "Letting her roam around this city on her own? So soon? She's going to go on her instincts. Many people will be killed," Bernadette warned.

"She can massacre all of Santa Monica for all I care. This state is too crowded anyway," he answered, tongue flicking Eve's wound; tickling her.

The old woman rolled her eyes. He was just like his father. Rash. Irresponsible Incredibly stupid.

"Those women will be the downfall of The House of Tyrell," she muttered as she went about her chores. She had always believed it was a mistake to have all those women in the mansion. What if they suddenly became jealous of each other? What if they escaped? Most of them had been locked up and had not had any human contact for so long that they were like animals. Now one of those animals was running around loose in one of the biggest cities in the world.

* * *

Eden was wandering around Griffith Park. It was a beautiful day. The sky was a soft pale baby blue and the fluffy virginal white clouds reminded her of the marshmallows her mother used to put in her hot chocolate when she was little. Holding onto a tree for balance she shook her head. That seemed a lifetime ago.

She squinted. Even though the bright sunlight burned like hell, it didn't kill her. A part of her almost wished it would. She didn't want to be an ugly monster for eternity.

Hiding in the underbrush she stared at the dozens of carefree hikers. She could hear their hearts pumping loudly in her ear. She could feel their blood coursing through their veins.

Her fangs throbbed lustfully, begging to tear through soft flesh and drain them. Eden growled and smiled as she imagined

11

the massacre; imagined blanketing Griffith Park in a shower of blood and corpses. Her tongue sensuously ran over her salivating fangs. It was just like being at a buffet. Her eyes darted back and forth, studying everyone as she wondered where she should start.

Carefree innocent laughter tickled her ears. Slowly she looked towards the noise and smiled.

A group of children were playing innocently on the playground. Their mothers, rich women who had nothing to do all day except gossip, watch TV and have affairs, were sitting at a picnic table engrossed in a tabloid as if it was The Bible. Every so often one of them would glance up to check on the kids; performing their motherly duties.

Eden chuckled as she sneaked closer to the playground. This would be like taking candy from a baby.

Eden had wrapped an old blanket around her body that she had salvaged from the trash. The blanket, a faded puce color, had been gnawed at by rats and there were several large holes scattered throughout. She had concealed her fangs with a delicate silk scarf with gold fringe; no doubt purchased on Rodeo Drive. In an ironic twist she had swiped the scarf from one of the mothers of the children she planned to eat for lunch. A bright pink and purple jump rope, forgotten and left on the grass, completed her image.

Her humming was what initially attracted the children. With wide eyes and open mouths they walked over to her, amazed by her jump rope skills. In their short lives they had never seen anyone jump so fast or for so long.

"Hi," she said turning to them.

"Hi," the children responded.

The stench of their young, innocent blood raped her nostrils, knocking her back. Her stomach growled. Her head pounded and it felt like her skull was caving in on itself. Her fangs began to salivate and her eyes twinkled lustfully.

"What are you doing out here?" A little boy with scraped knees and messy hair asked as he bravely took a step towards the stranger.

Eden smiled. "Looking for some new playmates," she hissed, her voice so shrill it sent chills up and down their young spines.

With one swift yank she ripped off the scarf and blanket revealing her monstrous form. The children's screams got lost in their throats and they froze with fright. Never in their worst nightmares could they have created the demon that stood before them.

Eden's eyes took on an unholy yellow glow that seemed to radiate from her pupils. The children tried to look away but her gaze was as hypnotic as a cobra's.

Eden smiled wider. She knew they were hers.

"Come," she cooed kneeling down. "Come to Eden."

The children obeyed her. On stiff legs they walked over to her. Eden's gaze fell over each of them. Smiling lovingly she caressed their cheeks and playfully tussled their hair. "You will be my sons and daughters."

Her eyes welled with melancholy tears. She had always wanted to be a mom. Besides acting, motherhood was her big dream.

Quickly blinking the wetness away she gave a quick little shake of her head, ridding her memory of the girl who had hopes and dreams and plans for the future. That girl was gone. Dead.

"Now," she continued, her voice acting as a lullaby and making the children sway. "Line up like good boys and girls and come to mommy."

A pretty little girl with dark red ringlets was the first to go. Her eyes were glassy. Cold. She, like the rest, had no idea what was about to happen.

Moving the girl's hair away from her neck, Eden wrapped

her hands around her small neck and penetrated her. Her highly acidic fangs dissolved through the girl's flesh. Now Eden knew why men loved to penetrate women so much. That feeling of being inside someone, of truly possessing them, was the greatest feeling in the world.

Closing her eyes in orgasmic bliss, Eden drank until the children lay around her, bodies an icy blue color.

Eden hissed, licking the blood from her lips. The children had been an amusing appetizer but she was far from satiated.

The pumping blood of joggers and hikers reverberated loudly in her ears. It was deafening. Icy, white hot pain slammed into her head. It felt like an ice pick was being jammed repeatedly into her brain. Moaning, Eden fell to the ground, clutching her head tightly between her hands. She squeezed her head tightly, needing to do something to alleviate the pain; not caring if she squashed her head like a grape.

Growling, she looked around, not caring who or what her next meal was.

* * *

"Oh my God! Where are the kids?!" One of the mothers screamed, looking around panicked.

The others looked around, motherly instincts finally taking over. None of them could remember the last time they had 'checked' on the kids.

Overcome with anxiety, the women spread out, praying to every saint and God they had ever heard of, and making a few up, that the kids would be found. They could feel their dyed hair transforming to gray and the stress wrinkles break free of their Botox.

One of the mothers left the trail and entered the thick trees calling the kid's names. Tears were running down her cheeks and it felt like she had swallowed a grapefruit whole.

Rounding into a clearing, she screamed. The children were lying on the ground in a hexagon shape. Some birds were pecking at their bodies. One had an eyeball securely in its beak and stared right at her.

"Oh God," she mumbled. Doubling over she retched. Monstrous heaves overtook her. A tight pain shot through her side and she wondered if she had broken a rib. Feeling hot bile burn her lungs she threw up until her stomach was empty. Her legs wobbled and she had to grab a branch to keep her balance.

Who could have done this?

She had to get out of there. It had suddenly gotten quiet. Too quiet. Even the annoying insects had ceased their buzzing.

Suddenly sharp talons dug into her shoulders drawing blood. She moaned out in pain.

Quickly the talons spun her around so fast she was dizzy. She gasped. Eden's smiling face was inches from hers. Her fangs were still dripping with the children's blood.

Without saying a word, Eden pounced. Wrapping her legs around the woman's waist she buried her face in her neck. The woman fell to the ground as Eden chewed through her neck, decapitating her.

Eden straddled her body, face buried in her neck. Ruby red blood was gushing from the severed arteries like a geyser, spilling onto the ground; staining the dirt a dark magenta. The woman's fingers twitched. Her head had rolled a few yards away from the body. Her eyes kept looking around confused and her mouth futilely tried to open and scream and beg the creature to stop.

A snapping twig made Eden look up. Her face was completely covered in blood. It ran down her cheeks and chin in a ruby river. She growled, angry at being disturbed. The other mothers stood in front of her; not believing what they saw was truly real.

Springing like a rattlesnake, Eden finished them quickly;

throwing their corpses next to their children when she was finished with them.

* * *

The two horny teen boys were leaning against the wall of the bathroom. This was their spot. They would steal their fathers' and older brothers' porn magazines, meet there and beat off. It was tradition.

"Dude look at her tits," one of them said. "They're huge!"

"Fuck man," the other one said, shoving the skin magazine he was holding under his best friend's nose. "Check out her pussy. It's pierced!"

"Oh shit. I wonder how that would feel against your dick."

"Dude, I can't wait until we lose our virginity. I wonder when we'll be able to see an actual live, nude woman."

"Right now," Eden's unholy voice startled them. She had been hiding on the roof of the bathroom gleefully spying on the teen perverts. "This is what a real woman looks like," she said seductively walking towards them.

The boys were shaking with fright. The porn had fallen to the ground, forgotten. They had instantly lost their hard-ons when they saw the demon.

"What's wrong?" She asked clutching their limpness tightly and making them rise up on their toes like ballet dancers; mouths open in a silent scream. "Performance anxiety? Don't worry boys," she soothed caressing their trembling cheeks. "It happens to all men. I always wanted to do a three-way." Smiling, she slowly leaned in and sucked them dry.

* * *

"Oh Julian," Bernadette called out too sweetly after rapping her knuckles against his open bedroom door.

16

"What is it now?" He asked. She was becoming a nuisance and he was contemplating burning her at the stake.

"You might want to put on the news," she responded with a slight smirk.

Julian turned on the news. A pretty black reporter was in the middle of Griffith Park. Blood and body parts littered the ground. It looked like a scene from a horror movie.

"To repeat," the reporter said, "Police are looking for any clues as to who or what is responsible for this horrific massacre that left no survivors. The LAPD have closed Griffith Park and are urging residents to keep their doors and windows locked. Police are also advising residents not to venture outdoors alone; even during the day."

Bernadette turned off the TV. "Looks like your new bride has had a busy day."

Julian chuckled. "Sadistic little cunt. I didn't think the bitch had it in her."

"This is serious Julian. She could expose us. They could kill you just like they killed your parents."

"Don't worry," Julian responded with a casual flick of his wrist. "I will take care of it."

The old witch's face puckered. Julian's way of taking care of it was to screw her as an award for murdering all those people. She had a bad feeling about this new bride. She was too feral. Too unpredictable. She had to be put down like a rabid dog. Not even Julian would dare massacre all those people like she had.

* * *

Julian sensed her before she climbed through the window.

"I saw the news. You had a very busy day."

"I was so hungry," Eden answered. "I needed to eat. But once I started I couldn't stop. Julian, you should have seen their

17

eyes! They feared me. I felt like a god."

"I'm not angry with you, my beautiful Garden of Eden," he said turning to her.

"You're not?" She asked, shocked.

"I'm quite proud of you." He lovingly caressed her cheek and kissed her forehead. Eden blushed and her heart beat with excitement. It meant the world to her that Julian was proud of her.

"Now my dear, you must bathe and dress for tonight. Some of the most influential people in Hollywood are coming here. So please, cover your fangs." He smiled and playfully chucked her under the chin.

Eden almost wept for joy. She couldn't wait for the party. She was feeling quite famished again...

A Discerning Palette
John Beck

"He isn't in." Rebecca hissed from between clenched teeth.

"Give him a chance. I just knocked. Look at the size of the place, he could be miles away." Mark waved a hand up at the massive edifice. Rebecca looked around nervously.

In the fading light of dusk the house looked ominous and oppressive. Rising within its own walled estate surrounded by new cheaply built properties, the mansion was a fading reminder of the majestic residence it had once been, standing proud and alone on the rolling green fields of the Surrey countryside. The lichen encrusted limestone walls stood lofty and incongruous within an oasis of overgrown lawns separated from the stark modern homes by a crumbling red brick wall.

"Knock again." Rebecca hopped from foot to foot as her impatience grew.

Mark passed the bottle of red wine he carried into his left hand then grabbed the black cast iron ring of the door knocker and released it with a resounding resonating deep metallic retort.

"How did you even meet someone who lives in a house like this?" Rebecca asked drawing her coat collar closer to her face.

"I told you. It was at the leisure centre. He saw me looking at the squash club notice board and we got chatting."

"Yeah, that's fine but inviting us both round for dinner. I mean, that's creepy."

"Rubbish. When he found out we live just the other side of the wall, he couldn't have been more friendly."

"Still, I think it's weird."

Any further comment was cut short when there was a clunk and the door swung inwards with a reluctant grinding that eased slightly as it opened fully to reveal a well dressed, middle

19

aged petit, man. His hair was immaculately brushed in a side parting and oiled. He wore a thin gray sweater over a pink shirt and light-blue tie. His dark brown trousers, predictably, were well ironed with crisp creases clearly visible.

"Mark. I'm so glad you could make it." He smiled as he shook hands with the younger, taller man. "And this must be Rebecca?" Rebecca hesitated before accepting his greeting and was slightly puzzled when he held on to her hand for just a second more than was appropriate. He held eye contact throughout and Rebecca noticed how deeply blue his eyes were, almost to the point of appearing violet.

"And you must be Milton?" Rebecca responded, holding his gaze.

"How remiss of me. Yes. Milton Crawford." He said bowing slightly as he introduced himself. "Do please come in." He gestured for them to enter and opened the grand oak door wider to reveal a large hallway beyond. Mark and Rebecca exchanged glances and entered the house.

The wide room rose all the way to the roof. The frame of the glazed dome that formed a canopy high above was now covered in verdigris. The glass was stained, cracked and neglected. The hallway itself was dimly lit and spartanly furnished. A hatstand with an umbrella hung alone and forlorn and was the only item standing on the antique poorly maintained wooden floor. A wide staircase rose majestically to a grandiose balcony containing many doors leading away to the landings on either side.

Directly facing the main entrance, stood a large window which, even at this late hour of the day, admitted sufficient illumination to eliminate the necessity of artificial light. Like the dome, the window, which once must have been a most imposing and impressive feature, was now tarnished and gloomy.

"This way please." Milton indicated that the couple should follow him to an open door to their left. In contrast to the growing obscurity of the hall, a warm glow emanated from the room beyond the half open doorway.

"The house is so difficult to maintain. One has always so many other things which demand attention."

"Excuse me?" Mark seemed genuinely puzzled. He had been glancing around, taking in the faded splendor of the mansion. Milton's comment had caught him off guard.

"I can imagine," offered Rebecca shooting her fiancé a warning glance and a frown that he knew meant, "Why should I be doing all the talking?"

"If you have no objections I would prefer to serve dinner in the kitchen. It's so much more intimate and personal. It will give us neighbors a chance to get to know each other." He smiled a broad sincere smile and led the way into the kitchen.

"For God's sake will you wake up," whispered Rebecca, her eyes narrowing in irritation.

"Sorry, Bex. After you."

Rebecca mouthed a brief profanity and followed their host through the doorway and into the kitchen, Mark trailed smirking.

The moment they entered the large open-plan room the delicate aroma of roasting meat assailed their senses. Mark's mouth watered and even Rebecca, an occasional vegetarian, found her appetite growing in anticipation. A large table dominated the centre of the room, beyond was another door, presumably to the outside.

On the wall to the right were two further doors. One was open to reveal a deep pantry, the other closed. The wall to their left contained the cooking area. An AGA stove and conventional gas oven stood side by side. Pans occupied the gas hob, bubbling and steaming merrily.

Milton stood by the table, his hands clasped, seemingly awaiting a reaction from his guests. When it became clear that Mark was content to keep silent, Rebecca forced a smile and approached their host.

"Well, thank you for inviting us along Mister Crawford..."

"Milton. Please." He continued to smile.

"Milton." Rebecca corrected.

"Not at all. It's always a pleasure to have guests, especially neighbors. Would you like to take a seat?" He gestured towards the large solid oak table. As Rebecca turned her attention to the table and the surrounding eight seats, she noticed for the first time that there were only two places set. She looked back to their host, puzzled, about to voice the obvious question.

"I'm afraid..." He paused. "...Rebecca." Again the smile. "That I love to cook, but have no appetite to accommodate my passion. So if you'll indulge me I would be honored to serve both you and your partner this evening."

Rebecca looked at Mark who shrugged. She could see that Mark was in one of his moods, why, she had no idea but he would suffer when they arrived home later.

"Not at all Milton, Mark's brought some wine." She indicated for her fiancé to present the bottle he carried. Milton accepted and studied the label.

"Australian. How lovely." He smiled thinly, Rebecca detected a little sarcasm. "I have a chilled Sancerre to accompany the appetizer but this will go wonderfully with the main course."

"Is that what we can smell?"

Milton's smile broadened. "Yes it is. A new recipe. My own. I am excited to see your reaction. But please sit, sit."

Mark pulled back a heavy wooden chair, the legs grating loudly on the stone floor. Milton stepped forward intercepting Rebecca as she reached for the chair beside her partner.

"Allow me." He effortlessly and noiselessly drew back the seat allowing Rebecca sufficient room.

"Thank you." She said sitting down. Rebecca was warming to this peculiar little man. "A gentlemen indeed," she added, glowering as Mark sat tight lipped and impassive.

"Good." Milton announced clapping his hands for emphasis. "An aperitif?"

"Love one." Mark announced giving Rebecca no time to answer. "Got any whisky?"

"Mark," Rebecca groaned.

"No it's fine. I do have an extensive selection of whiskies. But I would prefer to leave that for after, if you don't mind."

"Of course Milton," Rebecca agreed still staring at her sheepish fiancé.

"I have a delicate plum schnapps that may amuse?"

"That would be fine." Rebecca said with a nod. Milton gleefully turned his back and opened the cupboard door to reveal a wine rack.

"Amuse?" Mark whispered. Rebecca kicked him under the table, Mark winced.

Milton retuned with a bottle and two glasses. He withdrew the cork stopper with a satisfying pop and poured two generous measures of the purple liquid.

"You not joining us Milton?" asked Rebecca, as she savored the delicate fruity aroma of the liquid.

"Again I must gracefully decline. I have no real..." Again that pause. It was almost as though he had rejected the next word and was seeking another. "...stomach for alcohol." He finished.

"I bloody have," Mark laughed as he drained his glass in a single swallow.

Rebecca was sure she saw a pained expression cross their host's face for a brief second before the more familiar smile returned. She was compiling a list of Mark's misdemeanors and was running the opening lines of the row over in her head as she watched with embarrassment as her partner helped himself to another, larger glass of the schnapps. Rebecca sipped from her glass and was rewarded with a deep, yet fresh taste that was definitely plum but contained other more subtle flavors. The afterglow bloomed then faded leaving a satisfying warmth.

"Milton, that is very appealing."

"I am so glad. It's nearly a hundred years old," he informed, glancing at Mark who was pouring a third glass.

"And expensive no doubt," Rebecca speculated.

"Ah. I'd rather not discuss that. But yes, you wouldn't get much change from a thousand pounds for that bottle."

Mark paused and eyed his half full glass with new respect. Before he could speak, the little man had clapped his hands once more and scurried over to the gas oven.

"The appetizer is ready, but please give me a second to check the main course," he called over his shoulder. When he opened the oven door a cloud of vapor escaped, filling the kitchen with the most delicious aroma of roast meat.

Delicate spices hovered at the edge of perception and the overall smell lingered alluringly for a few seconds as he, with a satisfying nod, closed the door once more.

"What is that?" Muttered Rebecca absently.

"Oh, it's my new recipe. But I must keep it a secret. For now. Chef's prerogative." Milton was now by the fridge. He withdrew two plates and placed them in front of his guests.

"Voilà! Pâté," he declared with a flourish.

"And I believe that there was a mention of wine?" Mark declared hopefully to Rebecca's embarrassment.

"Of course. How rude of me." Milton returned to the fridge and produced a bottle, collecting a cooler and glasses from the adjacent unit. He uncorked the bottle and poured a small amount into a glass. Mark reached forward but Rebecca was swifter. She took a sip and nodded with an appreciative purse of her lips.

"That's really nice Milton." Before she could move to stop him, their host had topped up Mark's glass and poured a generous measure for Rebecca.

"Please enjoy." He motioned towards the plates with the Pâté and Melba toast then pulled out a chair opposite the couple and sat.

Throughout the brief entrée, his gaze never left either Mark or Rebecca; he watched one then the other as they devoured their appetizer. Whilst they ate, he spoke of their neighborhood with an uncanny knowledge of the recent past and of times well before the property developers moved in and constructed the hundreds of homes that now surrounded his estate.

"Don't you mind that the open land around your home is gone?" Rebecca asked as she finished the last of her pâté.

"Not at all. In fact, I've been here for so long on my own, I actually welcome the company. Hence tonight." He waved a hand towards Mark who was finishing the last of the Sancerre.

"Yeah, love it mate." Mark raised his glass enthusiastically, spilling wine onto his empty plate. His speech was slurred and his eyes were beginning to glaze. Rebecca groaned inwardly and considered making an excuse and leaving before Mark's state deteriorated any further. As if reading her mind, Milton shook his head slightly then clapped his hands once more as he suddenly stood up.

"Mark. Would you be so kind as to open the red wine? And I'll serve the main course."

"No problem." Mark muttered and struggled to his feet.

Milton handed Mark the bottle opener then returned to the oven. Rebecca looked on as Mark fumbled with the corkscrew, thankful that their host was preoccupied with the preparation of their main course. Finally after several attempts he managed to insert the opener and remove the cork.

"Voilà!" Mark exclaimed sarcastically, as he clumsily poured the wine. He waved the bottle at Rebecca.

"Pour me a small one. And I do mean a small one," she hissed acidly. "And I think that you should too."

"Rubbish." Mark slurred, taking a long drink of the wine.

Rebecca glanced at Milton who was busy serving the vegetables.

"Will you stop bloody drinking Mark; you're making a fool of yourself!"

"No I'm not. Milton's fine. Aren't you Milton?" Mark blurted far louder than was necessary. Milton glanced across, smiled and then nodded.

"See?" Mark sat back looking smug. Rebecca shook her head and narrowed her eyes; he was really going to suffer when they returned home.

Her malicious planning was interrupted when Milton opened the oven once more and the tantalizing aroma of their main course filled the room. The smell was unbelievable. Herbs and spices combined with the roasting meat made Rebecca's mouth water uncontrollably.

"Hurry up with that food Milton, it smells amazing." Mark shouted.

"I'm glad you are so enthusiastic Mark. It won't be a moment, I promise."

Milton removed the roast meat and carved it into steaks. Placing them onto plates with the vegetables, he carried the servings to the table and gently, almost reverently, placed the food in front of his guests.

"Thank you Milton, it looks fantastic," Rebecca declared inhaling deeply. The aroma was even more magical at closer range. The French beans, carrots and spinach were all well presented and added to the visual impact of the dish. Mark had said nothing but had instead tore into the thick, bloody steak with his cutlery. As he took the first bite, his eyes widened then his shoulders sagged as he succumbed to the taste.

"Milton, mate, this is something else." Mark chewed, half closing his eyes as if to focus and savor the experience. Rebecca sliced a small section from her steak and placed it in her mouth. Mark had not exaggerated, the meat contained flavors she had not experienced before. As she chewed the sensation increased and seemed to fill her with a glow not unlike the alcohol from the schnapps earlier.

"Milton, what is this? It's absolutely divine." She managed, with a whisper, as she eventually allowed herself to swallow the morsel.

Milton, now seated once more opposite the couple, beamed.

"It's my own recipe," he reiterated. "The secret is in the preparation and marinade of the meat."

"What is the meat?" Rebecca asked chewing another mouthful.

"A rather exotic cut. Maybe I'll show you later."

Mark had already finished the steak and, rather than eating the vegetables, had turned his attention to the bottle of red wine. Rebecca failed to notice, she was lost in the taste of the moment. Milton sat with his elbows on the table, resting his head in his hands contentedly, watching as Rebecca ate; she was oblivious to this attention. Mark finished the wine in his glass and reached for the bottle. His hand fell short and he slumped forward. He struggled to sit upright, and with the slow deliberate moves only the very drunk can achieve, he poured himself another full glass of the scarlet liquid.

Rebecca had now finished the steak and was finding that the delicate flavors of the vegetables were also a delight. Milton looked on, captivated. By the time Rebecca had finished her meal, Mark's head rested on his chest and he snored lightly.

"I cannot thank you enough for that experience Milton. I'm sure I'll never forget this."

"You are most welcome. That is very kind of you."

"I'm so sorry about Mark's behavior," she offered as she wiped her lips with a crisp, pristine napkin.

"Boys will be boys my dear. Think nothing of it."

"I appreciate that Milton."

"Now. Would you like dessert or would you like me to show

you the secret?"

"What secret?"

"The secret of my recipe."

"Of course. That would be wonderful." Rebecca felt genuinely curious.

"Let's leave Mark here, he seems very..." He paused, seemingly to consider his options, "...settled." He said finally, rising suddenly. "Please follow me." Milton crossed the room to the closed door beside the pantry, Rebecca followed. He opened the door and clicked a light switch to reveal a narrow stone staircase leading downwards into the gloom.

"Watch your step my dear. The stairs can be deceptively treacherous."

Rebecca followed as Milton started downwards. The strip lights above on the sloping ceiling barely penetrated the almost tangible darkness, making progress for Rebecca slow and uncertain. After climbing down a few dozen steps, Milton stopped.

"Almost there. When we reach the cellar please try to keep quiet."

Puzzled at this curious statement, Rebecca was about to answer with a question but Milton had continued onwards, she changed her mind and followed mutely.

At the base of the stairs was a small square room with rough stones forming the walls. Many strong lights blazed above brightly, illuminating the area. A large metal box hummed quietly in one corner, shiny and out of place. Rebecca placed a hand on the surface.

"It's cold," she whispered.

Milton nodded. "It's my fridge. I keep all of my meat in there." As he opened the door a cold cloud of chilled air escaped causing Rebecca to gasp. Inside the box she could see many joints of meat hanging amidst thick plastic strips. She could not, however discern what type of animal they were cut from. Milton closed the door with a sucking thud.

"The secret, my dear lies behind that door." He indicated a small metal opening that Rebecca had not previously noticed. A square slidable plate, rusty and ancient, sat in the upper half of the door and was closed. Milton withdrew the thick bolt and flung the door open.

"After you." He gestured for Rebecca to enter. For a moment she considered refusing but could not find any reason to do so. After all, her host had been kind and courteous all evening, even turning a blind eye to her partner's embarrassing activities.

"There's no light," she protested.

"Sorry. Of course." Milton flicked one of two switches on the wall beside the door. A single hanging light bulb came on, casting light on the room by the door only. Rebecca had to crouch to enter, a rank smell of rot and decay hit her like a blow. She gagged and turned to leave the room, as she did so, the door slammed and the hatch opened.

"Milton? What are you doing?" The stench almost made her retch.

"My secret. You remember?" He answered calmly.

"Yes. But what is that smell?" She looked over her shoulder into the dark imperceptible interior of the room. Had she seen something move?

"Oh that's Mister Garston."

"What? Who the hell is mister Garston?"

"The previous owner," he informed as though she should have known all along. "I bought the house from mister Garston and learned all about the property from him."

"I...I'm confused," Rebecca felt lost and alone, the calm demeanor of her host seemed completely out place considering her current situation.

"Can you open the door please Milton?"

"No, not really. It's my secret you see."

"What do you mean?" Rebecca could feel blind panic rising

within.

"Let me explain. In fact, wait a moment." There was a click and another stronger light came on to illuminate the remainder of the room. It was about the same size as the cellar and was empty apart from a pile of rags in the corner. As Rebecca became accustomed to the lighting she began to make out the shape of a man. The rags moved suddenly and a ghostly white face became evident. Rebecca wanted to scream but she was paralyzed.

"Mister Garston, I've brought you a visitor." Milton intoned with practiced pitch and resonance.

The rags unfolded to reveal the emaciated figure of a man. His eyes were red and bloodshot. His skin, like his face, was pale and hung in folds on a skeletal frame. He crouched staring at the young woman with hate and malice. His lips parted to reveal black, stained teeth, the canines however, were elongated and perfect.

"It's the preparation you see."

Mister Garston crept forward slowly on all fours. Layers of excrement and blood were encrusted and caked on his hands and feet. Rebecca found that she was unable to move. Opening her mouth to scream, she was stifled by terror, no sound came.

"Without blood, you see, the meat accepts the marinade so much more readily. It was a fantastic discovery."

The figure was almost within arms length now but still moved slowly and deliberately.

"I've kept him locked down here for nearly fifteen years. We've had so many guests, mostly neighbors. Thank you for coming." He slammed the hatch shut, leaving Rebecca alone with the horror in the cellar. An overpowering sensation of unreality gripped her as the figure leapt forward and began clawing at her face with talon like fingers. As the mouth of the nightmare closed around her face, reality returned like a heavy shroud of lead and despair. The beast bit down into her eye socket and she discovered that she was able to scream once more.

"Mark." Milton gently shook the sleeping man. "Mark." Milton said again louder, this time. His guest awoke.

"What?"

"You've been asleep for some time."

Mark sat up and blinked, unaware of his surroundings. For an instant he looked confused, then as his memory returned he forced a smile.

"Milton."

"Yes?"

"Where's Rebecca?"

"Oh. She's downstairs, I showed her the secret of my recipe."

"OK. It was very tasty." Mark was still drunk; a hangover however was slowly forming.

"Thank you." Milton responded with a genuine smile. "She said to bring you down."

"To see the secret?"

"Yes. To see the secret of my recipe."

A Long Ride
T. A. Branom

Something is odd with the stars tonight.

I take a quick look at Earth through my telescope then settle back on the Martian soil to watch the peculiar twinkling light show above.

A pink cloud drifts overhead in the night sky. It reminds me of pink puffy lips, like the lips of this steaming hot babe I met in a bar on my 35th birthday back on Earth. At the time, I wondered why such a sexy woman would be interested in a computer geek with long frizzy hair and thick-rimmed glasses. Knowing the why came too late. The way she spewed my name, "Mattheeewww," should have tipped me off that something was amiss.

The pink cloud slowly travels by, rounding off to a shape reminiscent of our biospheres here on Mars, and I think of Janie Maguire, the colony Captain's daughter. She works in the Ag dome growing crops. A real down-home girl. She even carries a 5-inch pocketknife. I'd love to bring her out here in the Martian night and sit between the big dish pointed toward Earth and the ERV, our Earth Return Vehicle, which I will one day pilot her home in. We could sit together with my little telescope and watch the pretty blue dot all night. I would most likely stare at her more than the heavens, ogling the way her wheat-colored hair curves against her delicate neck. But, she can't sit in the Martian landscape with nothing more than a hooded jacket as I can. And spacesuits are so bulky. Honestly, though, I can sit out here only because the ozone layer thickened enough to absorb a lot of the harsh UV. Otherwise, I probably wouldn't even be on Mars.

I pick myself up off the red Martian dirt, brush the seat of my pants, and peek through my telescope. There's a shimmer akin to heat waves rising from the red planet, distorting my entire field of vision in the eyepiece. I pull back, squeeze the corners of my eyes, and scratch my head. Mars doesn't produce sufficient heat yet for a shimmer like that. Steadying the scope, I peer through again. The stars ripple and flicker, disappear and reappear, as if an invisible dragon is flying through space. Maybe it's just my eyes. Squinting, I look for the blue dot that is Earth. The stars sway in a shimmering dance, and space opens up resembling curtains drawn for a play. Jagged fingers of lightning rip across the blackness not unlike an immense hand foraging for something. Brilliant light eddies to Earth and pools there, bathing the planet in a glowing emerald halo. Riding in the light is a colossal spaceship half as big as the planet and shining like a crystal sea of blood.

As space closes in the ship's wake, I sense...it. I say 'It', because it is not a crew in a ship but rather the crew is the ship. Melded. So many voices... So many souls, all searching in unison for the prey. I am weighed down by its want, by its need. I now recognize what it is seeking.

Humans.

A thrumming suddenly rumbles through me; a signal similar to a radar blip that only someone like me would know. I swallow hard and close my eyes. I imagine myself appearing as a green ghostly figure brightening and fading as I'm probed. A shiver runs up my back. I've been pinpointed. It knows how big I am. It knows what I am. Worse yet, it knows where I am.

Whatever is out there definitely isn't human. It's something ... like me. Not truly alive, but not actually dead, either.

And, it's hungry- starving.

I peek into the telescope again. The glow forms an angry cloud and billows around Earth. Lightning glows inside it, flickering with increasing intensity. I swear I see a face in the cloud--and it looks right at me. Light shoots from within the cloud, beaming into the solar system, and locating Mars. The flash through the eyepiece blinds me.

I stumble back and rub my eyes. I look up into space but see no sign of the beam. Grabbing the end of the telescope, I focus through it once more, only to find everything gone, and the familiar blue dot of Earth is only a pale, mottled rock resembling a big twin of the moon.

I step back from the scope and stare at the tiny speck in the sky, dumbstruck with the notion that life on Earth is most certainly gone. Furthermore, we won't even see this thing until it's too late.

As if whatever is out there heard me, blackness consumes the sky and blots out Earth; all the stars overhead suddenly disappear.

Is it coming for me? Is it coming for all of us? Survival instincts take over; my brain says flee. However, my heart says find Janie.

Leaving everything behind, I bolt inside the main biosphere. The halls are empty. No one knows yet. I twist side to side then rush to the Command Center.

As I enter, I hear static crackling over the speakers and I glance to the blank main screen. Captain Maguire sits with his head in his hands. Janie stands at his side, her hand caressing his shoulder.

"Houston. Come in, Houston." No reply.

The Captain pulls his daughter close to him. As only my kind can, I focus my hearing to catch his whisper. "Get to the ERV. I've already begun the remote start up. I'll be there if there's a problem."

"Come now." She wraps her arm around his. "You can be Captain from there. It's just a precaution. I'm sure nothing is wrong. Just a communication failure."

He smiles at her and pats her arm. "Get to the ERV. I have to organize everyone if something has happened." Her father turns his face from her. "I'll be there shortly. I promise."

Janie rests her forehead on her father's cheek. "I won't leave without you." She kisses her father and hurries from the Command Center.

Now I know for certain that I am the sole witness to what happened to Earth. No one else saw the spaceship, and the colony's main dish sees merely the blackness of space.

As I open my mouth to tell the Captain what I saw, I'm hit with the thrum again--like a distant whisper reminding me of who I am, and that I am the only one of my kind on Mars-maybe anywhere.

The spaceship is not just coming- it's here. There's too many people and too little time. I must save myself. I need only one human. Only one ship. Take Janie and get the hell off Mars.

I speed through the halls with all the inhuman power I can muster as I run after Janie. I catch up to her as she darts up the enclosed walkway and into the ERV.

Bounding up the walkway, I leap like a tiger into the ERV. I slide into the command seat and my fingers blaze over the controls, locking out the Captain's override authority and commencing lift-off.

"Wait for my father!" Janie screams.

"We can't wait," I reply calmly, not looking at her.

The door seals and the engines fire.

She throws herself around me to get to the controls, but I shove her into the other seat. She kicks at me, but I block every blow. Her vulgar screams drown in the rumble of the ERV engine. The upward force knocks her unconscious.

The radio blasts to life. Captain Maguire calls for his daughter. I click the speaker off. Mars falls behind the ERV, and a shimmer forms between the red planet and us. Our ship's lights and systems shut down as Janie and I plunge into glowing veins of radiant blue light flickering toward Mars.

The glimmering waves throb until the light condenses into a white ball that bursts like a balloon of sunshine. A giant ship appears flashing red, green, blue, and yellow repeatedly until it settles on the red--a deep, bloody red.

The thrumming hits me again, this time overpowering my senses, sapping me of strength and leaving me helpless in the seat. Whatever is in the ship is searching for more food...looming, hovering, craving. As tendrils from the red ship embrace the planet, I feel a fevered roar from the entity as it sucks the energy from Mars along with all the life on it. The pulse deepens inside me, rising in pitch. The vibration rumbles every cell in my body. It's unbearable, like I'm about to come apart. Oh, how I wish I were unconscious like Janie.

I scream, and it's over.

The red ship heaves like a relieved lover, undulating slowly with satisfaction. Then there is a silence as if the entire universe is hushed. I feel so...alone. I glance at Janie still passed out in the seat, her hair sticking to the dried tears on her cheeks. I reach out and pull back her hair.

The ship outside blazes bright white and the tendrils fold around it like cradling arms. With a glittering burst, it's gone.

Mars appears as a pale red ghost of itself--blotched and drained. There will be no more pink clouds floating in the Martian sky. No more sitting with my little telescope and watching the pretty blue dot all night.

Nevertheless, Janie and I are still here. I don't know how or why- maybe we weren't enough for 'It' to notice. Maybe it didn't want us. Maybe it left us on purpose, since, in all probability, we are the last of our respective kinds.

With that, I know there's no longer a point to hiding and no reason for subtleties.

"Janie," I whisper and shake her gently.

She leans forward, eyeing the planet as she blinks herself awake. "Where is my father? Where is everyone?" She begins to shake and her breaths quicken. "You," she hisses through clenched teeth as she fights back tears.

I stare at the floor. "Janie, there's something I need to tell you."

She snaps her head toward me; her brows pushed together, the lines on her forehead deepening to a V, her eyes darkening. She clutches the ends of the armrests as if she is about to jump at me. "You son of a…"

"Janie," I close my eyes. "I'm a vampire."

Janie gapes at me, her eyes wide. Words lodge somewhere in her long, beautiful throat. She pushes back in the seat, her face wrinkling in disgust and confusion.

"Don't worry. We need each other to stay alive." I know my words offer no comfort, if she even hears anything that I say at all. I gaze out at the stars. "I'm perfectly suited for a long, cold ride in space." I swallow hard. "That is, of course, if I have something to drink."

Janie's lips quiver, but her eyes flare with loathing, not fear.

"I will use the ship's artificial blood for as long as it lasts. That's what I've been using anyway." I peek over at her. "But, if it comes down to it- if I need to take from you- please know that humans don't notice a little blood missing here or there. You replenish it quickly enough."

Her face scrunches and her teeth grind together. "So, I become a vampire?"

I smile a little at the question. "No. If I'm a vampire and you're a vampire, we'll both die." I focus back on space. "You need me to fly. I need you to live." Janie's shoulders slump, and she closes her eyes. "I'll only need to take a bare minimum to survive. The food and water are yours."

Bowing her head, Janie Maguire nods as if she understands.

"We'll make it," I say with confidence. "I promise."

Janie lets out a small sigh and pulls her hair back for me. Her artery pulses hard. Slowly, I bow to her neck only for a kiss.

Her hand jams against my ribs, her knife slicing open my skin. Blood oozes onto my shirt. I flop backward into the command chair.

"That's for my father!" Janie's face is like a savage dog; her nose curls upward in a sneer. With a twist and a hard jerk, she yanks the knife out. My life drips from the end of her blade. I sit up, snatch in a mouthful of air, and squint into her fury.

"Janie. Oh, my dear Janie." I open the tear in my shirt enough to reveal the wound. The gash closes neatly leaving only the slightest divot where it had been. Janie's smirk sags and her pupils dilate. She doesn't even breathe.

I pounce upon Janie, my teeth sinking into her soft neck. My mouth cups her flesh, but I let her go as quickly, letting her slump like a rag doll. She wilts into the seat, stunned, her eyes still wide. The first bite is always a shocker to a human. Janie's lips tremble with voiceless words.

I stand and lean over her. "That was for us." I fetch some ties and bind Janie's hands and feet. "We need each other to survive." I pause, my mouth only a breath from hers. Her scent churns my thirst. She turns her head and closes her eyes, holding back her anguish, her despair, and her contempt for me.

"We WILL make it, Janie." I power up the ERV and set a course toward Earth. Maybe I'll find a fully stocked blood bank for me. Nevertheless, I need to find extra food for Janie. Maybe some canned stuff. Keeping her alive is my priority.

It is going to be a very long ride.

A Pound of Flesh
Ken Goldman

Outside the 2-Street Tavern a misty drizzle washed the avenue and the dim light from the bar cast misshapen reflections in murky puddles. It would take more than a rain storm to wash the sidewalks of Queen's Village clean, and old Josh knew he could do nothing about the blood spilled in the street wars occurring regularly outside his tap room. But inside, that was another matter. Inside a man had some control over the craziness that smoked the sidewalks beyond the tavern's doors.

The storm had kept most of the regulars home and the place was practically empty. Behind the bar Josh took one look at young Skeezer Woolsey coming out of the rain and knew that some very nasty shit had gone down in those streets tonight.

Skeezer found his usual stool vacant directly in front of the Miller tap, but even seated the young man seemed unsteady. He sat there soaking wet, the blood on his face smeared by the rain. Josh pulled out a towel. Moistening it he handed it to Woolsey.

"Did George Foreman just tap dance on your face, man? I've seen dog turds that look a whole lot better than you."

The young street warrior mopped his face with the towel but beads of sweat still dotted his dark skin. The right sleeve of his denim jacket was ripped from his shoulder, clinging loosely to his arm by a half dozen stitches. A thick meaty gash of torn flesh practically halved the young man's cheek as if someone had tried slicing through it with a can opener. The zigzagging crimson smear extended to Skeezer's chin.

"You and your corner boys been fuckin' with them pavement junkies from the North Side again, ain't that so?" the old man asked. "Sweet Jesus, man, you gon' to wind up just like them worthless Clayton Brothers."

Everyone in Queen's Village knew that story. The twin

brothers, each ugly as dried wood, had divided their adolescence between raising hell and dealing drugs. Last summer both of them suddenly disappeared from the Queen V without a trace. People in the Village figured someone must have given those twins a new home on the bottom of the North End River. No one much cared to pursue the matter.

"Just hit that tap, will you, Joshua? And don't stop hittin' it 'till I tell you. This ain't been a real good night."

The bartender had already pressed down the tap handle before Woolsey spoke, but Skeezer seemed too whipped to notice. Josh watched him chug-a-lug his beer in quick gulps without the mug leaving his lips. He waited before speaking, figuring anything he might say before those suds were inside the young man's belly just wasted his breath.

"Now, Skeeze, I know you ain't got nothin' in your pockets worth rollin' you into no alley for, seein' as you ain't held no steady job for as long as I known you. And you ain't dumb enough to go sniffin' after she-stuff that don't belong to you. So I figure there must be somethin' else goin' down between you and whoever done that mess to your face."

As was his custom Josh exercised his right to know as much of anyone's business he cared to ask. Sliding another mug in front of Skeezer, the old man moved his chair to the stool near the Miller tap. "You ain't goin' to be no endorsement to do much drinkin' here lookin' like ground hamburger. So maybe you feel like tellin' me a piece of your story 'count of the business you costin' me?"

Skeezer shifted on his stool like something clammy had just crawled up his ass. "You want a piece of the story, old man?" he asked, unable to even smirk at Josh's dubious logic of the youth's repelling customers inside an empty bar. "Okay, that's cool. I'll show you one big piece of it right here."

He held open his jacket just wide enough to reveal the small .22 in his pocket. "Finally got the chance to use my rod tonight, old man. Been waitin' a long time."

Rebuttoning the denim and dabbing the towel against his cheek he did not have to ask the bartender for his third brew. He held the mug steady with both hands, a man coiled so tight Josh thought his guts might explode right inside him.

"You don't want to be tellin' me you killed a man with that gun, Skeezer Woolsey. A God fearin' man like myself might not want to hear a thing like that." The barkeep was no fool. God was not all he feared. He knew about those things no one should know about, and he knew just how much he wanted to know about them. In the Queen V a smart man understood when to stay stupid. Josh had no idea about what happened to the Clayton brothers, and he didn't want to know. Maybe the prudent thing now was to exercise his right not to know too much about Skeezer Woolsey either.

Skeezer leaned toward him, his voice almost a whisper. "Ain't no man I killed, Joshua, I can tell you that. You remember J-Bird, usually came in here on Monday nights to watch the football game?"

J-Bird. Old Josh always expected to see that little crack head hemstitched with a semi-automatic one day. He was an ugly biscuit-skinned street punk, incapable of attracting anything but flies. But J-Bird and Skeezer were corner boys. As far as Josh knew, Skeezer had no bone to pick with him even if he was one mean-assed mother grabber whose street name boasted a rap sheet that spread from where Josh sat to the curb.

"That crack-dealin' nappy-headed lump of tar?" Josh asked. "The skinny monkey that used to borrow quarters from me for the juke box to play 'Heard it Through the Grapevine' 'bout sixty-three times a night? Yeah, I remember him. So?"

"So I think maybe J-Bird heard somethin' through that grapevine, all right. Somethin' that made that man real uncomfortable," Skeezer said, lighting a Chesterfield and letting it hang from his lip while he spoke. "J-Bird and me wasn't as close as me and the Clayton brothers, Joshua, but we wasn't 'zactly strangers either. That's how I know the man I run into tonight wasn't the same J-Bird. I seen him over on Third Avenue and when I call to him he acts like he just fucked my mama, then keeps right on walkin'. 'Hey, man!' I yell out, but he just hauls ass like he's got some 'pointment he's late for. Right then I know that mo'fuck dropped a dime on me to those Queen V junkers he carryin' for and decided he don't know me no more."

In Queen's Village the street was your family and you sooner would have your testicles torn off before you fingered your own corner boy. But not every corner boy played by that rule. Josh wasn't surprised that J-Bird chose to save his own ass by giving the Judas kiss to Skeezer. That's the kind of trash he was.

A piercing thunderclap interrupted his thoughts, followed by a bolt of lightning that tore a crevice through the sky. Lights inside the 2-Street flickered with the grumbles of thunder. Although startled, Josh felt grateful for the brief distraction. He had heard so many variations of Woolsey's story of betrayal from corner boys going back thirty years, and he could almost mouth the words along with him.

One-time bloods sometimes turned on each other for no sane reason. But tonight someone had kicked the crud out of this young buck, someone who had put a real chill into his heart. Anyone capable of spooking Skeezer Woolsey that bad immediately spooked the old barkeep too.

"Storm's not over," Josh said absently. "We lose power in here, the taps go warm an' I might as well be servin' my customers piss." But Woolsey was too far into his tale to give a rat's ass about Josh's taps.

"J-Bird always be messin' where he shouldn't," he continued, the cigarette doing a mad dance in his mouth. "He got me into some bad shit carryin' for the junkers 'cause we wasn't deliverin' nothin' with anchovies on it. Last week J-Bird says to me, 'Skeeze, this powder we got in our pockets is worth somethin' on the street, and ain't no buyer gon' to miss a few grams here, a few grams there.' I tell him I don't want no part of that mess 'cause these are bad mothers to fuck with. That night I stopped playin' the game and wouldn't carry their shit no more, so I don't see J-Bird for a few days. But J-Bird, he keeps deliverin' the cola for them, and every night he shaves off a little cee here and a little cee there hopin' no one catches on. I know that blow monkey got hisself way over his head this time and someone must've knew they was bein' shortchanged. Turns out I was right, too. J-Bird needed some dumbjohn to point the finger at, and that lyin' mo'fuck decided to tag me ."

The door opened and a lone stranger walked in, his pale face half hidden by the high collar of his raincoat. Skeezer looked over his shoulder to watch as the tall man walked to a booth at the other end of the bar and sat with his back toward them. Outsiders rarely frequented the 2-Street, but the rain had become heavy again and likely the guy just wanted to get out of it. Josh thought it odd the stranger did not remove his wet coat, but he didn't intend to bring anything unusual to Woolsey's attention that might unhinge him even more. The outsider turned to look at them but turned quickly away.

A man comes into a bar, that man ought to order a drink, Josh thought. Nights in Queen's Village always seemed filled with things that made no sense.

"That piece you got in your pocket," the bartender continued. "Any of those slugs find their way into J-Bird tonight?" The old man felt uncomfortable with his question, but Skeezer Woolsey carried something more evil inside him than the .22 in his jacket, something he wanted to get out.

"I need another beer, Joshua. I can't remember when I felt this thirsty."

Josh placed a tall frosty mug in front of him, but Woolsey just looked at it, so lost in his thoughts that he did not touch it.

"I emptied the whole chamber into that cocksuck," Skeezer

said, stubbing out his cigarette and quickly lighting another. Woolsey leaned forward, as if sharing a secret. "But it ain't what you think, old man. I didn't do it 'cause that fucksnake dimed on me, but 'cause what I seen in J-Bird's face just wasn't right. When he don't answer me I run up to him and spin him around. 'Hey, man, I'm talkin' to you!' I yell right at him, 'So maybe you got somethin' to say before I take my pound of flesh out of your black ass?'

"He turns an' looks right at me, Joshua, and I'm lookin' into J-Bird's face like I seen it for the first time. He's gone milky white, white as if his mama was fucked in a Georgia bale of hay. That ain't the worst of it. The man don't say a word, just hisses at me like he's a goddamn snake! Then he shows these teeth --- Shit, man! Those teeth didn't belong nowhere 'cept in a dog's mouth... or maybe in somethin' a whole lot worse..."

Josh had not anticipated Skeezer's wild curve. The barman considered telling him he had heard enough for tonight, that maybe Skeeze had sniffed one line too many with his boys. But Woolsey's voice had taken on the tone of a confession and the old bartender knew his tap room was as close to church as the young man was ever going to get. He said nothing.

"J-Bird comes for me with his mouth wide open like he's gon' to take a piece right out of my throat with those teeth. I'm backin' off sayin' to him, 'Listen, J-Bird. Forget this shit. You an' me, we go way back. Ain't no need to--' , but then he's suddenly on me, bitin' at my face with those teeth. I know he's got no intention of talkin' it over with me. Damn, I can kickbox the shit out of that rust-faced sucker, but tonight he's suddenly got the juice of fifty men and I know he ain't about to stop 'til he done some serious damage. I feel I'm wrestlin' with a fuckin' cougar the way he's all over me. So I pull out my piece and shove it right into J-Bird's face. 'Take some advice, motherfucker, and back off right now or I'm gon' to blow those teeth out the back of your head !' But he don't hear. He jus' keeps comin' at me. So

46

I fire - - - Bam! Bam! Bam! - - - I'm pumpin' slugs into his white bread face until it ain't there no more and I got nothin' left to squeeze off. After that, I just run, leavin' him for the sewer rats to finish and the law to toe tag. I tell you, Joshua. Whatever it was that I pumped lead into tonight, it ain't the J-Bird I used to know!"

Josh considered his next words carefully. A God fearing man had to say them. "You killed a man tonight, Skeezer Woolsey. You got to do the right thing now. You hear me talkin' to you?"

Skeezer did not look at him, and when he finally spoke he sounded like he might choke on his words. "Yeah, old man. I hear you."

A sudden thunderbolt exploded outside and thick veins of lightning split the night sky. The avenue strobed while the ceiling lights inside the 2-Street blinked off, then back on. They went off again and stayed off. Outside the street lamps flickered, silence filled the tavern and it lingered in the darkness. The door swung open then slammed shut. It happened again, then a third time. Tiny winks of lightning cast ghostlike shadows around the tap room. Someone had come in, maybe several people, and something moved inside that had not been there before.

Josh stumbled in the dark toward the drawer near the freezer for candles, and scratched a match to light one. In the flickering light formless shapes moved toward the bar counter like dark specters. He strained to see but could not make them out. Looters maybe. Power failures always sent them crawling out from their crevices like night vermin, and Josh stood near the cash register where he kept his handgun for just such a confrontation. It would not be the first time he had used it.

"Now you hold it right there so's I can get a look at you!" Josh called out to the shadowy figures who approached.

The old man held the candle straight out before him while Skeezer Woolsey sat like a stiff corpse. The firelight glimmering

47

in the young tough's eyes caused Woolsey to turn away from it. Josh caught a glimpse of his face and suddenly the old man's mouth fell open. "Oh, sweet Jesus! Oh sweet mother of Chri--"

Now, without seeing them, Josh knew the dark figures surrounding his counter were not looters. Looking at Skeezer Woolsey he knew his visitors were something worse, something much worse.

A voice near him whispered. "You know what's in here with you, don't you, old man? You do know..."

Skeezer Woolsey's eyes glowed in the dim candlelight like charcoal embers. Other eyes glowed in the darkness all around him, many other eyes.

"A candle ain't 'sposed to give off so much light," Skeezer said, his voice almost childlike with misbelief. "I know it's dark in here but I can see you plain as day, Joshua. I can see everything in here like it's tomorrow mornin'. Shit, man, what's happenin' to- -?" He shut himself up, and Josh knew why. Because Skeezer Woolsey could see through the darkness ...and because he could see who was inside the tavern with them!

Someone near the counter had spoken, but the young man remained paralyzed on his stool. The voice sounded like nothing belonging to the streets of Queen's Village. Josh held out the candle to the man's pale face.

Before him stood the same stranger who had entered earlier. His lips curled in a tight smile while his mouth displayed teeth that were much too sharp and impossibly white to belong to anything human.

"Mister D.!" Skeezer said. "Shit, Joshua, I know this man! J-Bird and me, we done business with this man!"

"True, true," the tall stranger responded still smiling broadly while his eyes fixed on Woolsey. "And business is what brings me here tonight, my young friend." The man still had not removed the rain soaked trench coat he wore but even so he looked insanely delicate alongside Skeezer. In the winking candlelight thin veins threaded through the pallid flesh of the stranger's temples. The flesh seemed old and sickly, but his face was not that of an old man. He turned to the shadowy figures among the many behind him.

"Business, in fact, is what brings all of us here," he added as if this were a signal. The tavern door opened once again and a lanky figure stepped in from the night, then slowly made its way to the bar counter.

There was something familiar about the way he walked, something so familiar...

"J-Bird!" Skeezer said even before the figure stepped into the firelight. The youth's flesh seemed like something made of paper and thick paste. Two of Skeezer's .22 slugs remained lodged in each cheek, and one had cracked the bone of his chin. Blood-caked teeth curled over his thick lower lip. He looked like a kid wearing some grotesque party mask bought in a cheap costume shop, an insane mixture of an urban street kid and a corpse.

"Just look at me, Skeeze. You fucked me up good," he said. The ridiculous greeting seemed wildly incongruous, as if some stinking clotted creature had crawled from its grave to ask Woolsey the time.

Another two shadowy figures stepped closer to the bar and in the dim candlelight Josh recognized them too. The Clayton brothers!

"How you doin', old man? It's been a while," B.B. Clayton said to Josh, then turned to Woolsey and added, "Hey, Skeeze."

Simple. So simple it was insane.

B.B.'s dark skin had gone purple, and it glistened with either sweat or slime, Josh could not tell in the firelight. The old man held the candle out to see better, but B.B. pulled away from it as if shielding himself from a burning sun.

"I don't think you want to do that again, old man," B.B. said, wearing the same shit-eating grin Josh had remembered. But it really was not the same. Not the same at all.

The quiet brother, Duane, stood alongside his twin, his front tooth still missing. But now there were new teeth, and they looked very sharp.

"Take a good look at us, Skeezer," J-Bird said. "The Claytons, me, and all the rest in here. We ain't real pleasant to see, but we all fuckin' VIPs 'round this town! We workin' for the man, Skeeze, and we the baddest asses in the Queen!"

"I see you, all right, J-Bird!" Skeezer said fear and rage spidering veins through his temples. "And I seen you earlier too when you chewed at my face like you was some pit bull hungry enough to eat the ass hole out of a bear! That weren't no bad-assed mo'fuck I saw earlier, J-Bird. That was some kind of snap case demon, one whipped up crazy- -"

"Not crazy, Skeeze - hungry. That's what you saw. You gon' to tell me you don't know somethin' 'bout that kind of hunger, Skeeze?" J-Bird turned to the Clayton Brothers. "Ain't too many of us in here who ain't felt the hunger of that sweet tooth habit. It comes and it goes, Skeeze... but there ain't no real need for me to be tellin' you all this, is there?"

B.B. stepped forward. "'Course there's hunger... and then again, there's thirst. Thirst so bad you feel like you got cotton balls in your throat..."

Their laughter was the mad screeching of ravenous animals, and the tall stranger who called himself Mister D. raised his hand to quiet them. He leaned toward Josh.

"Who are you?" Josh asked. "Who the hell are--?"

The stranger spoke low as if sharing a secret only the old bartender might understand.

"You heard the young turk, Joshua. I'm 'The Man'. A businessman, to be exact. Not every drug habit is satisfied by a line of powder up one's nose or the prick of a hypodermic needle. I'm talking about simple economics, my friend. A vampire's law of supply and demand is no different than any entrepreneur's. A gram of cocaine, a gram of flesh and blood... it's all the same.

I have simply found my market, established my territory, and provided my services. I would conduct my trade right here on this corner just like you if I could. But my line of work, by its nature, must of necessity remain somewhat secretive if I am to stay solvent. The Clayton boy here tells me you've had this establishment on this same corner in Queen's Village for over thirty years?"

"Thirty-four," Josh added. "But I don't see what that's got –"

The stranger's eyes shone in the darkness as if some inner light glowed inside his skull like a sickly jack-o'lantern's.

"We all do what we must to survive, Joshua. You rely on your clientele as do I, and we each do our part to quench the thirst of our customers. But in my case, Joshua, I create the demand for my supply, just as any dealer must. And there is only one certain way to create the demand for blood, the thirst for it! My market far surpasses those foolish venders of crack cocaine - because consumers of blood do not die! The vampire is the perfect consumer because he creates more consumers like himself, and my business increases exponentially! I'm sure you understand, old man. Business is business."

"Then you're no different than those gone-to-hell cruds in them crack houses down the block," Josh said.

"No, Joshua," the tall man amended. "I am different. Their profits result in the deaths of boys like these. Mine result in their eternal life!"

J-Bird took this as his cue and seated himself on the stool alongside Skeezer. He placed his hand on Woolsey's shoulder, the one with the torn sleeve.

"Listen to Mr. D., Skeeze, and he'll quench that thirst for you like he does the rest of us. All you got to do is recruit some more. That's what we was doin' all along anyway. We wasn't deliverin' powder for Mister D., Skeeze. Oh, yeah, there was cola in them bags, but that wasn't what the dude wanted to push. The coke was just a front to fool us, man, and them buyers didn't give a shit that I was appropriatin' their snow, 'long as we sold enough to cover expenses for what we was really unloadin'. Man, you and me went dancin' every night into their vampire turf, and it was the cee that made us believe the man was just doin' some business. Cocaine ain't worth squat to a vampire... but blood is another matter when you be talkin' 'bout street prices."

"You ain't gon' to get no rush like that from reefer or orange cap crack!" B.B. Clayton added. He could not stop laughing.

"You'd shit green if you saw the foldin' jack a vampire's likely to be carryin' in his pockets, Skeeze," J-Bird continued. "Think on it, man. We was deliverin' bags of coke to buyers who was sendin' all that cee right back into the streets. 'Cause what them leeches really wanted was some boyz in the 'hood! A vampire's got connections you can't even dream 'bout, man, and he glad to pay top dollar to suck up all that premium gravy comin' fresh from a young dude's vein. And we delivered it right to their door step, man! Streets be too violent even for a vampire these days, Skeeze, and wantin' to keep a low profile they don't want no mess with no Kojaks or someone knows somethin' 'bout defendin' hisself in a dark alley. Thanks to us no blood suckers don't need to worry 'bout huntin' the streets to feed their habit, long as they got the cash. You an' me was scouts recruitin' more Queen V corner boys to be feedin' D.'s payin' customers' blood habit. People with the habit always come up with the jack, and D. knows that sure as any junker that comes to this part of town. Sell the coke, buy the blood, and Mr. D. collects his profits. Need more buyers? Then create more vampires. It's free enterprise at its finest, man, 'cept the boys carryin' the goods don't know it's themselves they 'ventually be sellin'!"

J-Bird looked at the tall, pale man with an expression of reverence oddly co-mingled with fear. "The man's a pro, Skeeze, a real flesh peddler, and he got contacts everywhere. When Mister D. here uses up one place the dude moves on to some other urban feedin' ground in some other city. He don't need to worry 'bout no shortage of suppliers, and those suppliers soon gon' to create even more demand. Now there's a lesson in economics I ain't never understood 'till I worked for the man."

B.B. moved closer to Woolsey, so close that their faces nearly touched. "And now it looks like we gon' to move on to another town too. We got to go with him, Skeeze."

"We?" Skeezer asked.

"Let me show you how it is." He yanked Skeezer's denim collar down to expose his neck. Skeezer instinctively felt there for the two deep holes that still leaked blood, holes that J-Bird had bitten earlier that evening as he and Woolsey had struggled on the wet sidewalks. The bites had pierced a thick vein in Woolsey's dark skin, but now that skin had begun to go pale.

He ran his hand along his cheek searching for the shredded flesh of the wound that had been there earlier. Already the laceration had practically healed. But the skin felt cold, like raw meat.

"You see what I'm sayin'? You dead, man. But then again, you ain't."

"I'm thirsty," Skeezer said, licking his dried lips.

Josh looked at the last mug he had poured for Skeezer Woolsey over fifteen minutes earlier. Woolsey had not even touched it. His was not that kind of thirst.

The crazy thing was that to Josh, Skeezer Woolsey looked a damn sight better than he had one hour earlier... even with two elongated fangs protruding from his purple gums. Skeezer rose to his feet and faced the bartender.

"These streets ain't no place to be without my corner boys, Joshua. B.B.'s right, man. I see what I got to do. You understand what I'm sayin'?"

"Yeah. Yeah. I understand," the old man said.

The terrible truth was that he did.

53

* * *

Moments later they were gone.

Josh sat behind the counter inside his empty tavern without moving for almost an hour. The flame from the solitary candle on the counter fluttered in his eyes.

The candle had gone to a nub and Josh waited for it to flicker out. He did not feel much like lighting another one. Maybe he couldn't do anything about the craziness that walked the streets of Queen's Village but a man behind these doors had at least some control. If he wanted it to remain dark inside his tavern then he could see that it did.

It was almost 1:30 a.m., still thirty minutes before last call. Power failure or not, nothing would make Joshua close shop for the night.

A young couple walked in.

"Didn't think you'd be open, the power bein' out," the man said. He snapped his umbrella shut and handed it to the woman while he removed his coat. "Damn messy out there, and everything else is closed. Must be a slow night, huh?"

Joshua smiled. Maybe he would light another candle after all. "Always slow on a rainy night like this. Beer?"

A Vampire Song
Aline S. Iniestra

Smoke and blue light
Wrapped him on the stage.
A black suit and sunglasses
Hid his true essence.

Playing sensual notes
And moving to the beat
Christian caught my eyes
Only fixed on him.

As he turned to look at me
I glimpsed his sharpened fangs
Making me surrender
To a twisted yet sweet smile.

His hands on the keyboard
Played a song of love
I was dancing to his movements
Asking for a lot more.

Silence, Lights out.
Hands clapping and holler.
I stood still in the dark.
A cold breath on my shoulder.

Just one second and I bled
As he bit me in such a bliss
I was drawn into his arms
This was music to my ears.

Two vampires danced and kissed
To the smoke and blue light
To the blood we shared
To the music of the night.

Wicked nightmares were to come
I had thought it was devotion
I was only one more prey
I had been my own destruction.

An immortal made by Christian
When he had been wrongly named
All I wanted was perpetual love
Now I'm left alone, in pain.

But my anger was too strong
And I chased him for a thousand years
Now he knew what a true vampire was
I gladly bled his useless life away.

While we danced at a gloomy club
I bit him as a sensual foreplay
When he was ready for the action
I slit his neck. He agonizingly prayed.

"No one will hear you
This place is too wicked
Your eternal enamored fan
Never deserved such a maker."

And the dance floor became red
With Christian's ancient blood
And I danced next to him
Singing a vengeance song.

Johnathan
Nate D. Burleigh

Chimes echoed through the house sending mounds of goose-flesh racing up Kit's spine. With his head tucked between his legs, he tried to control the hyperventilating. Because in his heart he knew what needed to be done; what had to be done. The fear had to be gulped down and he needed to suck it up and answer the door.

The chair skimmed across hardwood as he pushed himself away from the computer desk. He cinched up on the 9 iron sitting in his lap until his hands shook from the strain, or the terror, he couldn't tell which. What lay beyond the threshold of his home, beyond the oak front door, had tormented him for hours, or had it been days? Where time began and ended had become a blur amidst the intimidation. But now it had to end and he needed to end it.

"Just stand up, Kit. Walk to the door and open it. You can do that, can't you?" The incessant pleading of the chimes sounded. He jumped, startled. Even though he knew to expect it. And it would happen again and again until he mustered the courage to face the man standing on the front stoop. If that's what he was.

Kit stood. His knees knocked within his designer jeans as he shuffled toward the front door. Sweat poured from his brow and a tear raced down his cheek. He clasped the handle, raised the club, took a deep breath, and faced his fear.

* * *

On most days Kit worked from home, but on occasion (as it had been that day), they would have mandatory in-office meetings that required him to be there in person. On those days he would load up on his anti-anxiety pills and force himself to leave the house. His partner usually took him to work on these rare occasions. But Brett had gone to Salem on business and wouldn't be back until later that night. Which meant that Kit would have to either drive or ride the bus. And because driving in town scared him worse than being around people, he'd opted to take the express bus from Vancouver into downtown Portland.

On his way to work the digital clock in the dashboard read 7:25. "Shit! I'm gonna miss the bus." He applied more pressure to the gas pedal and the neon-green 86' Cabriolet backfired as it hit seventy, careening down the wet freeway. He had about fifteen minutes before the medicine kicked in. Plenty of time to make it to the transit center.

If he'd gone to sleep at a decent hour he wouldn't have been so late. But he rarely got to sleep before two or three in the morning. His nights were fraught with horrific images: heads bumping down stairs, hideous creatures crunching bones, ghouls attacking children underwater. The plagues of his mind came to fruition every night as he slouched in front of his nineteen inch monitor. When his mind swam with ideas, he'd work until either his hands hurt so bad he had to stop, or his eyelids became heavy enough that he couldn't lift them anymore. That's how the nights were for the budding writer of speculative fiction.

The car came to a screaming halt at the red light. Dread filled him as the 199 bus drove by. He pounded his open palms against the steering wheel and cursed under his breath. Now he had to wait for the next bus, which meant he would probably be late for work.

When he pulled into the lot at the 99th street Transit Center, people had just started gathering on the side of the bus. He sprinted to the back of the line, edging out an elderly woman who he saw speed walking for the same spot. A smirk scrawled across his face as he climbed on board and realized his favorite seat (the corner seat by the window at the back of the bus) wasn't occupied. Perpendicular to his spot sat a bench seat with a metal bar behind it that made for a handy footrest. He'd just settled in, placed his headphones in his ears, and raised his foot to the bar when a man plopped down on the bench seat.

The middle-aged man smiled at nobody and dug into his soft briefcase. He pulled out a little bag of chocolate doughnuts, stuffed one into his mouth, took a swig of his coffee, turned and said, "Shhhhhhh, don't tell anyone."

Kit smiled and crossed his heart.

"I love these things," the man said and pushed another one into his mouth. "You want one?"

"No, thanks. I don't do so well with food this early," Kit said, scrunching as far into his corner as he could.

The man held out his hand. "Name's Johnathan Cunningham."

Kit hesitated and then took the outstretched hand thinking it would be warm and greasy, but withdrew when it turned out to be cold and dry.

"You got a name, kid?"

"Kit."

Johnathan stretched his arm over the seat and twisted his body. "That's an interesting name," he said.

Shit. He wants to talk, Kit thought. Once the meds kicked in he would be okay with a friendly conversation. However, that hadn't happened yet and his nerves were firing times ten. He took a deep breath.

The man looked at him with a quizzical glint in his eye.

Kit removed his Ear-Bud headphones in an effort to be polite. "It's a nickname," he answered.

"So, what's your real name?"

"Everyone just calls me, Kit."

"Well, Kit..." he said with a pleasant grin. "This bus go downtown Vancouver?"

"No. That's the 105." Kit looked at his watch. "If you want

that one, you'd better hurry, it leaves in a couple of minutes."

"Nope, this is the one I want." Johnathan smiled and his pudgy cheeks pushed against the bottom of his large oval glasses. A pungent odor akin to stale public-restroom cologne wafted in the air about him. A full head of dark-gray hair settled against the collar of his white shirt. The solid-blue necktie he wore dove straight down his chest and then whooshed up over his belly like a tiny roller coaster. Ending his ensemble, were neatly pressed khaki pants that stopped four or five inches short of a pair of white wing-tipped loafers. Fashion faux pas, Kit thought. Though he'd been surprised to see that the man had worn black socks.

"So, what do you do in Portland?" Kit asked.

"Oh, I usually work from home, but today I need to go in for a meeting." He swigged some of his coffee.

That really hadn't answered Kit's question. "Me too," he said.

"You too what?"

"Usually work from home."

"Oh. Then we're kindred spirits." Johnathan said and stuffed another doughnut into his mouth, offering one to Kit with a gesture.

Kit held up his hand, politely declining the offer. "Do you like working from home?" He asked.

"Sure. It gives me more time to write my books."

That piqued Kit's interest. "What kind of books do you write?"

"Mostly computer texts. I'm a computer programmer by trade. Also got a book of poems published. Been meaning to start a children's story. But right now, I'm working on a physics book. Got some new ideas I want to introduce to the world."

Kit decided to gleam some more info from the published author to see if he could learn anything about the business.

Johnathan rambled on about how he came up with the idea

for his children's story. This didn't interest Kit, though, it did lend for an opportune time to let the man know he too had aspirations of becoming an author.

Kit interrupted, "I have a children's story published at sleepy time dot com."

"Really?" Johnathan asked.

"Yeah, it's called 'Kiera and the Moon Queen'."

"I'll have to look it up. Do you have anything else published?"

"Several stories in various online magazines and a few horror anthologies."

Johnathan went silent. His bright smile collapsed into an emotionless line. At that exact moment it seemed as though dark rainclouds covered the rays that had been warming them through the east windows of the bus. He cocked his head to the side and Kit could have sworn he saw flickers of red light in his eyes.

"I thought you wrote stories for children?" Johnathan said slow and methodical.

"No. That's the only children's story I've ever written. I write horror, speculative fiction."

Johnathan's eyes tightened and his brow furrowed. "You better be careful writing things of that nature."

"Oh, I am." Kit smirked.

"No. I'm serious." Johnathan moved his bag from his right side to his left and scooted closer. Leaning over the rail of the bench, he whispered, "very serious."

"Sure." Kit shrugged. "Why so serious?"

"It's evil."

"What's evil?"

"Delving into that which you don't understand."

"Like?"

"Evil! Dirty! Benevolent! Horrible! Trash!"

Kit smiled, not knowing what to say.

Johnathan didn't look amused. "If you write evil, you invite evil into your life. Heed this warning. Be very careful, lest you become possessed by the very thing that you wish to become famous for. I've seen it happen. Some can get rid of the evil, but most end up in the looney bin...or worse."

"What can be worse?"

"Dead," he whispered, staring deep into Kit's eyes.

The sincerity of those words ripped into him as if he were being gutted with a buck knife. Kit gulped. "I'll be sure to keep that in mind."

"I mean it," Johnathan said, not breaking his glare.

The bus squealed to a halt as it pulled up to Kit's stop. Johnathan swept up his bag and waddled to the door; apparently, also his stop. "You might not want to forget that," he pointed at Kit before he got up from his seat.

Crazy talk. The man is absolutely out of his mind, Kit thought. But the little prickles scampering across his neck made him think otherwise. They departed the bus. Johnathan went left and Kit went right. While Kit waited for the crosswalk light to turn, he noticed Johnathan creep back onto the bus. Must have forgotten something, Kit thought.

After the all office meeting, he stayed and worked disability claims at the insurance company for eight more hours. Once the day ended, he almost had to crawl onto the bus, and this time, someone had taken his favorite seat. At every stop on the way home he watched for the lunatic technical writer, dreading the moment he would step into the isle. Relief washed over him like a cool breeze on a summer evening when he made it back to the transit center without encountering the man.

The sun had receded and the desolate parking lot screamed, "mug me." With glances to the left and right and several over his shoulder, he jogged to his car and sped home.

Where's Brett? He thought as he pulled down the dirt driveway. Usually his partner's car would be parked next to the front gate under a patch of pine trees. He pulled into his spot and got out.

The ranch style home sat on 1.2 acres of lawn with some scattered pine, oak, and a couple of apple trees. They'd purchased the place so they could be away from people. Kit didn't do well surrounded by a lot of people.

In the kitchen he found a note on the refrigerator door.

Gone to Portland for a late meeting. Don't forget to get something to eat. See you when I get home. Love you...Brett.

Home alone. A propitious time to work on his novel. The screen flickered to life. He opened the word document containing his novel and the blank page stared at him. He'd been in a bit of a funk with the story line, but after meeting the stranger on the bus, his head filled with many fresh ideas.

Kit had a niche in his story telling. He liked to use his co-workers names as characters. It had been something he started doing early on and they really got a kick out of reading about their untimely demise, usually in a most horrific fashion.

The next scene had a particularly gruesome moment in it. Tim Haskins (one of his co-workers with a bit part in the novel) was walking home from a kegger totally wasted. The killer drove by in a supped up '69 Chevy Malibu and held a machete out the window. It connected at the base of Tim's skull. Instead of slicing straight through the neck, the razor sharp blade cocked upward, exiting through the eyes. The killer laughed as he watched half of the man's head slide off through the rear view mirror. Kit wrote until he fell into a stupor.

He awoke with his face plastered to the keyboard, drool slimming the 'asdf' keys. There were four thousand pages of gibberish on the screen and scrolling up to where he actually stopped writing took quite a while. The computer's clock read 9:30 PM. His bladder felt like it would explode any minute and when he stood, a clanking noise drew his gaze down. On the floor, with its tip covered in blood, sat a three-foot long machete. Mind numbing horror overcame him and he sat, staring at the blood soaked blade.

"What the hell?"

The computer monitor flickered and his Windows Media player opened. A movie started to play. The digital image looked like it came from the window of a car. Whoever held the camera panned down to the machete sitting in their lap.

Kit gasped as he realized those jeans were the same ones he had on at that very moment.

The car crept behind a man walking down the street with his hands stuffed deep in his pockets. Kit knew that slouch anywhere. He'd even emailed Tim a tip that he found online that noted if he put a piece of tape between his shoulder blades, every time he felt the tape get tight, it would signify his slouching. Apparently, it hadn't worked.

"No! This can't be happening." Kit shook his head as the person in the car set the video recorder down and picked up the machete. The engine revved and the screen went black.

"What the hell was that?" He turned and looked at the macabre tool smearing blood on the floor of his office.

"Get a grip, Kit. You're tired, imagining things and possibly losing your damn mind," he said, staring at himself in the black screen while the computer rebooted. When he looked down, his assumption had been correct, the blade; and blood, were gone. He let out a long sigh of relief.

After tapping in his password, the desktop came back up and the computer recovered the novel. Satisfied he hadn't lost any of the great scene he'd written, he began the next chapter.

Melena, Tim's grieving widow, thought she knew who the killer might be and decided to confront her ex husband, Jeremy. She found him with his throat torn out, lying on the kitchen floor in a pool of blood.

His cell phone went off with the smooth sound of Kenny G. He leapt to his feet and searched his coat pocket. "Hello?" He said after clicking the green button, but the caller had dropped. He shrugged it off. Moments later the phone beeped. Someone sent a text. It read: 'I told you not to forget it. LOL...John.'

"What the...?" Johnathan had somehow acquired his cell number. What else could he have gotten a hold of? He did say that he was some sort of computer genius. Maybe he'd tapped into Kit's computer and read his story? Then faked the video, or worse?

An email popped up and he instinctively clicked on it. The URL of the local news channel blinked on the page. The email didn't have a subject and wasn't one he recognized. But curiosity got the better of him and he decided to check it out. He clicked on the News Chanel 8 link and it brought him to a live web feed. A reporter stood in front of a line of police tape. The caption at the bottom read, 'Breaking News'. Kit turned up the volume.

"We can now tell you the identity of the man found dead at the corner of Charleston and Northwest 99 in Beaverton. Tim Haskins, a local man that worked in downtown Portland for a prominent insurance company, has been killed. Police will not comment on how the death occurred. We can only speculate that it was a hit and run. They will neither confirm, nor deny foul play."

Blood rushed to his head and Kit felt faint. He couldn't help but think that by writing his story, he'd gotten a co-worker killed. It began eating away at his insides like salt on a slug. The crazy bastard, Kit thought. He did this. Or, was Kit actually becoming possessed by his own dark words? Like the insane son-of-a-bitch had said. His mind wondered in and out of scenarios and every time he came to the same conclusion, Johnathan had to be behind it all. Kit decided to call the phone number that had popped up earlier on his phone to test his theory.

"Hey there. You've reached, John. I'm not available to answer the phone right now. You know what to do after the beep."

Now with the email and phone call as evidence, Kit knew who the perpetrator was. The man had hacked into his computer, read his story, and killed poor Tim. Thinking he might be next on the killer's list, Kit got up and retrieved his 9 iron from the closet.

It then donned on him that when people read the story they would think that he'd done it. The thought of spending the rest of his life in prison for a murder he didn't commit made his stomach lurch. He pulled up the document and erased the chapter. "There. Now where's your evidence?" He smiled at his cleverness. At any minute the man could show up brandishing the machete. But he'd prepared himself. Armed with the golf club, and a new resolve to do anything necessary to survive, he waited.

* * *

Kit staggered to the front door with his hands clenched tight around the golf club. The bell rang again and he jumped. Then his cell went off.

The text read: 'I'm at the door. I have something for you.'

He knew that on the other side of the door their stood a machete wielding psychopath who would stop at nothing to take his head. He wiped sweat from his forehead and peaked through the peep hole in the door. Johnathan stood with his back turned and began whistling an eerie tune. If Kit reacted fast, he could open the door and get a blow in before Johnathan knew what hit him. He turned the knob slow, making sure not to make a sound, and then swung the door open as hard as he could.

Johnathan whipped around. His bared teeth had a sinister glow in the dim porch light and something in his right hand glinted.

Johnathan

Kit didn't have time to gawk. He brought the 9 iron down dead center of Johnathan's forehead. Skin split open and the skull cracked under the pressure. Kit pulled the golf club out of the man's head and Johnathan fell to his knees, looking up in bewilderment as blood flowed down his face. Kit didn't want to take any chances and swung the club as if he wanted to knock a ball a hundred and fifty yards. It struck under Johnathan's double chin, crushing his windpipe. On the follow through, blood, spittle, and fractured teeth sprayed into the air. His arms flailed as he fell backwards, cracking his head against the cold concrete path.

Kit's breaths came in quick slurps and he dropped to his knees, the world swimming around him. He looked around for the machete. Then he noticed something in the man's right hand and crawled over to the outstretched appendage. Horror etched into every crevice of his face, the hair on his arms and neck stood on end, and he slapped both hands to his forehead.

"How could I be so stupid?" He looked back over at the blood speckled right hand. "He was just trying to return my property."

Kit thought about the phone call and the text messages and it all made perfect sense. That's what Johnathan meant when he told him not to forget it on the bus. Then, bless his soul, he got back on the bus to retrieve it. "What have I done?" He said over and over, sobbing into his hands.

"Kit," he heard from behind and whipped around to see Brett standing over the body. "What's this?"

"I fucked up, Brett. I killed him. All...all he wanted was to give me my wallet. See it there in his hand?"

Brett crouched and examined the wallet. Then he scooted next to Kit and embraced him. "It's okay, sweetie."

"I thought he was stalking me. He said some weird shit on the bus this morning and I took it to heart."

"It's okay. You didn't know what you were doing."

"He had me going. There was an email and a text. And...and this video on the screen. The machete!" Kit yelled.

"You were hallucinating again," Brett said. His always soothing voice calming Kit.

"Really?" Kit sniffed.

"You know this happens when you go too long between meals."

"I know," Kit said, wiping blood and tears from his face.

"Well look there. You don't even have to hunt, your food came to you, see?" Brett pointed at the bludgeoned man's body.

"I hadn't thought of it that way," Kit said.

"I'm sorry I left without bringing you something to eat first. Now look at you. After all of these years of not wanting to hunt on your own, you finally did it. You took a human life. That wasn't so bad was it?"

Kit brushed more tears out of his eyes, smiled and said, "I guess not."

"That's my boy. Now, to get you some nourishment." Brett's eyes burned deep crimson. He opened his mouth, revealing several rows of jagged, razor sharp teeth.

Kit's mouth tingled as his own teeth splintered to life.

Brett reached over, grabbed a handful of Johnathan's hair, and dragged him between the two. "You first," he said.

Johnathan jerked and his eyes opened. Terror stretched across his face like a plastic bag, suffocating.

"Great, he's still alive." Brett twisted the man's head until the side of his neck bulged in front of Kit. "I know how much you hate this part," he said and slid his fingernail through the layers of fat until it pierced the jugular vein.

Johnathan coughed and gagged.

"Bon appétit," Brett said.

Kit placed his mouth over the gash.

Johnathan's eyes made frantic left and right glances as Kit slurped and lapped at the blood flowing from the wound.

Johnathan

Brett sunk his teeth into the left wrist making Johnathan squirm and whimper.

Kit watched the death grip on his wallet relax. As the hand fell limp and Johnathan took his last agonal breath. Kit thought, I'll have to remember not to wait so long between feedings.

Blood Family
Christopher Hivner

The tall one was gentle while he tied the family up. He wore no shirt and white-streaked blue jeans. Wavy, brown hair fell over his back as if he were the singer in a rock band. His wide, angular shoulders rippled with muscle as he tightened the ropes on the kneeling father, mother, and teenage daughter.

The shorter, slimmer man, dressed in a dark blue track suit and brown work boots, peered at them with one eye as the other was covered with a 'V' of dirty blond hair. After the family was tied up, he went to them one at a time, backhanding their faces, throwing vile words at them like jagged rocks, enjoying the fear in their eyes. The mother held fast, but the daughter cried. The short man flicked a pink tongue out, licking the tears from the girl's face.

Another round of blows were coming until a third man walked through the front door. Dressed in a black pinstriped suit with a vest and perfectly knotted silver tie, he moved with an overpowering confidence. The other two men now stood shoulder to shoulder in the shadows of the room, their eyes on him but directed to the floor. The new man's sandy brown hair was professionally styled, cut short and parted on the left side. He walked over to the father and posed with his hands behind his back.

"Look at me," he said. The father tilted his head up, meeting the man's gaze.

"My name is Maxwell, and I believe you know why we're here." He waited for the father to speak but was met by silence. Maxwell sighed. "Please, Mr. Durning, you know how this will end. Don't force me."

Albert Durning lowered his head again, squirming in his ropes. "He's not here," he finally said.

Maxwell smiled. "Let us see," he sang in a jangly voice. He walked behind the tethered family, placing a hand on the father's balding head. "Mr. Albert Durning is present." He moved to his left and put a hand on top of the mother's head. "Mrs. Amanda Durning is present." The daughter shrank as Maxwell's hand covered her auburn hair. "And Miss Michelle Durning is present." Maxwell then laughed. "So the entire family is present this evening... except five-year-old Master Tyler Durning. Tell me Albert, where does a toddler go after dark in your neighborhood?" The only reply was Michelle's quiet sobbing.

Maxwell walked over to the father and knelt down, leaning close to the man's face. "The world doesn't keep secrets. All the families know of him and will be coming; we're just the first. If you somehow survive this night, how will you vanquish all of us?"

"He's a child!" Mrs. Durning suddenly yelled. Maxwell turned to meet her rage-filled eyes. "How can you people be so heartless? Leave him alone!"

Maxwell reached out a manicured hand to cup Mrs. Durning's face. "A woman this lovely cannot possibly be so naïve. You know what we are, and you know what your son is." Maxwell stood up and began to pace. "The first human child in the history of the world to be born immortal, and the mother doesn't understand all the fuss. 'Just let our boy grow up like a normal person. Leave him alone.'"

Moving with a grace that belied his size, Maxwell leapt at Amanda Durning, grabbing a fistful of her hair and yanking her head back.

"The first human...to be born...immortal," he growled. "His blood is priceless, and I mean to have it. WHERE IS HE?" Maxwell opened his mouth, peeling back his lips to reveal curved, yellow fangs. He pressed their points into Amanda's cheeks, roaring in violent anger.

The room had become a cacophony of feral sounds: Maxwell's bellowing, Amanda's screaming, her husband's pleading, and the daughter's crying.

Over top of all, it came from the corner of the room, the tall intruder's soft exclamation of "What the hell?"

Maxwell looked at him quizzically, seeing him gazing at the ceiling. Twisting his head around, he looked up and directly above him saw Tyler Durning, naked and covered in a downy black hair. He hung from the stucco by the talons emerging from his fingers and toes. Then he dropped.

Before Maxwell could completely turn, he took slashes to his face and chest, and then the child was gone. He pressed two fingers to his cheek. They came away dripping with blood. His two companions were quickly at his side, the shock pooled in their wide eyes.

"Did you see where he went?" Maxwell asked them.

"No," the shorter one replied. "He was too fast. You said..." The complaint was cut short by Maxwell's bared teeth and vicious stare. "Dancer, you go to the basement. Taj, upstairs. I'll stay on the main floor. Find him."

The tall man opened the basement door while Taj swallowed hard before running up the stairs. Maxwell pulled a handkerchief from his vest pocket to wipe the blood from his face.

"He's farther advanced than I thought he'd be," he said to the father.

"You have no idea."

Maxwell turned around angrily, thinking he was being challenged, but he saw each member of the Durning family slumped together, breathing in concomitance.

"When did he start?" He asked. The father answered again.

"Six months."

"Did you...?"

Albert Durning shook his head. "We're not like you, you know that. What he does, it's inherent."

Maxwell fingered the slice in his shirt and the barely-there scratch on his skin. The boy had moved with such speed that Maxwell never saw the thrusts coming, only felt the pain after. It proved how powerful his blood was, but it also gave Maxwell pause. His clan was meager: Dancer and Taj were young and inexperienced, and he was feeling his own strength wane. He needed that blood. After 450 years, this was his first chance for real power.

The living room was small: a few pieces of furniture, a door leading to the basement and another to the kitchen. The staircase was twenty steps going up at a forty-five degree angle, open to the room.

Learning from his previous underestimation of the boy, Maxwell scanned every square of the ceiling. Satisfied he wasn't going to be attacked from above again, he started with the furniture. Bracing himself, he turned the couch over then moved quickly to the love seat. Met only by dirt and loose change, Maxwell grabbed the last piece of furniture, a single-person chair, and flung it across the room to quell his growing frustration.

"Where are you, boy?" Maxwell bellowed. He threw open the door to the kitchen, stalking around the island in the middle, wildly pulling open the cupboard doors. Then he heard a crash from beneath. He stared at the tile floor. There were more muffled bangs, followed by screams. There was a thump, and the floor directly in front of him rose up.

Maxwell raced back into the living room and to the basement, hesitating a moment before pulling the door open and stepping aside. Carefully Maxwell eased his head around the door jamb to stare into the darkness. He bared his teeth with a guttural growl, morphing his fingers into crusted, black talons. Not sensing any imminent danger, he stepped into the gloom.

Taking each step slowly, Maxwell was hit by a myriad of odors: mold, oil, cat urine, stale barely-breathable air. At the bottom of the stairs was a square cement landing. He turned to his left and dropped a foot to the uneven basement floor. Under the stairs was a perfect hiding place, but he didn't detect any movement, breathing, or human musk.

To his left Maxwell could see a rusted set of metal shelves holding paint and household cleaners. To the right were a washer and dryer. Ahead was a door to the outside and a dog leg into the corner that was underneath the kitchen.

"Dance? Where are you?" The basement was silent.

"Boy? Come out and face me." No sound.

Maxwell strode purposefully across the room, turning to face the blackness of the rear section. He immediately smelled blood. "Dance," he whispered to himself.

The odor struck him from manifold directions. It was strong at eye level a few feet ahead, but also a light sense of it pierced his nose from each side, and there was a pungent hit from his feet. Maxwell stretched his right leg out. His foot soon felt an object. Bending down, his hand wrapped around the handle of three foot long trimming shears. The blades were covered in blood. Maxwell licked a thick dollop into his mouth. It was Dancer's.

"Boy!" He railed in anguish. Suddenly the light bulb that was inches from Maxwell's head flickered on, and he was looking into Dancer's eyes. They remained open, ice-blue orbs gazing out from his head that hung by a chain off of a wooden ceiling beam. Then the basement door slammed shut.

Maxwell's own eyes burned orange-red. His breaths came in deep, hard gasps as he stared at his friend, asking himself just how powerful the Durning boy might be, only five and taking down an adult immortal with ease. Maxwell seethed. He had to have that blood. To be anything in his world you had to be powerful. He was tired of impotence, tired of the low ground. He wanted respect.

The door above opened. Maxwell turned in full attack mode and soon found himself with his hands around Taj's throat. The smaller man bent to his knees fighting for air. Maxwell slashed his spikes across Taj's face then lifted Taj into the air with one hand.

"Where is he?"

"I don't, knknkn, can't… breathe. I don't kknoww."

Maxwell loosened his grip around Taj's throat. "Where is he, Taj?" Taj just shook his head.

"Dancer is dead," Maxwell said. "And we're next. That boy, oh, that boy is stronger than I expected. His blood will more than rejuvenate me. It will exalt me. I will rise to heights I never imagined." Taj was dropped to the floor again.

"He's so much more than I had dreamed. I couldn't even sense his presence. Do you understand what that means? The power!" Maxwell peered down imperiously at Taj. "Get up! We'll start on sweet sister and see if he gives a damn about his dull, mortal sibling."

"We can't," Taj said fearfully. Maxwell's teeth were piercing his skin by the time he finished. "They're gone!"

"What?"

"When I came down from searching upstairs, they were gone. The ropes are lying on the floor."

"Go!" Maxwell shoved Taj onto the steps. Stealing a glance backward into Maxwell's blackening eyes, Taj felt his body stiffen. He knew he would be destroyed either way, because Maxwell had no intention of sharing the boy's blood. Taj's only chance was to get out of the house while Maxwell and the boy fought.

Taj was still formulating his escape when he reached the top of the stairs and came face to face with Tyler Durning. The boy hovered in the air, the color in his eyes dancing like a bonfire. Taj could feel the heat emanating from the boy's presence. He remained mesmerized until the sharpened point of the curtain dowel rod penetrated his skin and burst through his heart.

Taj instinctively grabbed at the weapon as his breath caught in his throat. A distinctive black circle appeared at the edge of his vision, slowly narrowing to a singular point. Taj's mind spun backward madly until he was a child again, standing on the porch of the old farmhouse. His sister, smiling broadly in a new flower print Sunday dress, held his hand. He was dressed in gray short pants, a white shirt, and his only pair of shoes. Out in the yard of hardened dirt and dust, his mother called his real name, Charles, trying to get him to smile. He snuck a look at his impatient father waiting in the buggy with the horses wondering when they were going to get to move. One more coaxing call of his name and Taj smiled meekly for the man with the giant camera. He squealed, "Mommy" before falling backward down the basement steps.

Maxwell deftly leapt up, grabbing hold of a wooden beam, allowing Taj to pass beneath him. When he dropped back down, he looked at the deflating body fluttering as the life force escaped. He peeked at the basement door to see the boy watching him.

"You have another of them for me?" Maxwell said with a laugh as he walked up the stairs. "My heart's going to be tougher to get to."

Maxwell went airborne, flying through the doorway. His outstretched hands reached for the boy's neck, but at the last second Tyler eased sideways and with just a touch of his fingers sent Maxwell tumbling across the room. He crashed through the ornate, wooden railing of the upstairs steps, bouncing off the wall.

Tyler Durning hovered over the prone vampire, incandescent wings flapping at an invisible speed. Knowing Maxwell wasn't dead, the boy watched at what he thought was a safe distance, determining his next move. But before he could act, Maxwell sat up, eyes now obsidian rocks. He opened his mouth and erupted in a howl that spewed sulfurous breath into the boy, knocking him head over heels to the floor. Momentarily stunned, Tyler lay on the deep-pile, champagne-colored carpeting taking labored breaths. Then his body rose into the air as Maxwell had gained control. The vampire spun the boy around faster and faster, slashing at him with his diamond-hard talons. His body shivered when he thought of how Tyler's blood was going to taste, how it would feel coursing through his veins, the power it would give him, like nothing he had ever possessed. Maxwell tilted his head back and laughed from his ancient belly.

"The time has come," he said, his voice an octave lower, raspy like boiling water. "Your power will be mine, boy."

Maxwell stopped the spinning child and left him hanging in mid-air. Tyler Durning's body was limp, covered in scratches and cuts, blood flowing in spatters. Maxwell reached out a finger for a drop when the boy's eyes snapped open and one of the broken bars from the wooden railing was shoved into Maxwell's back and out through his heart.

The vampire dropped to his knees. Behind him, Dancer's headless body held onto the make-shift stake, pushing it in deeper. Tyler Durning held up a tiny hand and Dancer stopped. The boy eased down in front of Maxwell who spoke with desperation.

"How?" He asked, his eyes rolled back in his head looking at Dancer's body being controlled by the child.

"I can do things," Tyler answered, "more than others."

"It doesn't... ha... have to end... this way. We can wo... work...together. Help me. Make... me...strong. I'll...follow."

Tyler pointed to a large portrait photo on the far wall of his father, mother, sister and himself sitting in front of a fake beach back drop. Tyler's face bloomed with the silly grin of a five-year-old, happily sitting on his big sister's lap while his parents stood over them like protecting angels.

"My family," Tyler said to Maxwell.

"Isn't over. There...will...be others," Maxwell said. Tyler

leaned closer.

"Sending them a message," he said then nodded. Dancer shoved the stake another foot through Maxwell's eviscerated heart until the body collapsed. Tyler stared at Maxwell, peering into his mind. He gathered the names of all the immortals from Maxwell's memory and swirled them together in his own thoughts, creating a miasma of faces and histories. He could see that many of them were indeed on their way.

The boy sent out a wave that emanated in his brain and shuddered through his whole body. He directed it to every clan. Only moments passed before they answered. Tyler was connected to his kind for the first time, but there were few that were happy about it. He told them Maxwell's story, announced the death of the family. Those that wanted his blood were not deterred. Then the boy opened his mouth and spoke aloud.

"Come and get me."

. . . Of the Night
Lyle Perez-Tinics

Once upon a horrid dream,
Moonlit beams that I redeem.

Walking alone as someone follows me,
Wind blows; a shiver grows as I flee.

Turning around, not making a sound,
I feel my heart stop, feel my soul drop.

Someone glows afar, like a distant star, running toward me.
Someone so bizarre grabs my head with hands of dread,
My eyes close as my neck turns red.

I awake I'm different I am numb.
What have I become?

Hubert Humphrey: Vampire Extraordinaire

David Bernstein

Hubert Humphrey was not evil, unlike many of his kind. He was turned by his own choosing. As a human, Hubert was picked on for most of his life; from school bullies to the corporate jerks in his law firm. He was lanky and small in stature, resembling a man made of fuzzy pipe cleaners. One night after leaving work, he was mugged. Stabbed and beaten; left like road-kill for the maggots.

Martyre, a vampire from the mid 19th century, had been strolling the alleyway looking for a meal when he came upon Hubert and his attackers. He slaughtered them wickedly, saving Hubert from immanent death.

"Such a pity," Martyre said.

Hubert, through one semi-open eye (the other mashed in by a boot heal) had managed to see Martyre's actions.

The stranger had torn through the men like they were nothing more than papier-mâché dolls. As inhuman as Hubert's savior had seemed, his mind accepted what he witnessed.

"Not sure you're going to make it," the stranger said.

"Thank... you," Hubert managed, unable to move.

"Think nothing of it."

"Call, 9, 1...1," Hubert whispered. His breathing was shallow and getting worse as his right lung filled with blood. A nauseating gurgle came from the puncture wound in his chest.

"No time for calls, it's live or die time my friend," the man said. Hubert felt numb, as if the ground was quickly freezing under him. At least the men, who had hurt and ultimately killed him, were dead. He wouldn't have to fret about haunting the area where he died. His killers had been brought to justice.

"My...wallet. Take...the cash... it's yours," Hubert said. It was the only thing he could think of to properly repay the man for what he did.

The stranger bent low, whispering in Hubert's ear. "Time to live, or time to die, my friend. What's it going to be?"

"Live," Hubert said, bewildered.

"Do you wish to be like myself? Powerful by night, weak by day? To feed on the undeserving, each day thirsting for blood? To live throughout all of time, watching the mortal ones die off?"

"Yes," Hubert said, and closed his eyes knowing at that moment what the stranger was.

"My name is, Martyre, I will be your Sire." Hubert's life force was taken, sucked to the point of death before feeding on Martyre's own tainted blood.

Hubert had thought his life would be easier; have a better quality to it, but after his master was killed (only three weeks after being turned himself) by hunters, he was left alone. He had to make acquaintances on his own, and was often ignored or made fun of. The vampire world wasn't much different from the human one as far as social order was concerned. Hubert was, as when he was human, still seen as awkward, fragile, and weak and his philosophy on undead life kept him at odds with most of his kind.

Martyre was a typical vampire, feeding on whoever crossed his path. Hubert disliked him, but it was how the majority of bloodsuckers lived.

As a vampire, Hubert had the same approach to living as he did when he was human: Let live, leave alone, and mind one's own business. He'd taken his fair share of innocent human lives, but never could get the feeling of dread off himself after a kill. It must have been the humanity left in him.

As a former criminal defense attorney, (went missing and presumed dead according the police) Hubert kept up with local court cases. He watched the news with eager consistency night after night, and scoured the internet for cases where the innocent were robbed of justice. He went after the guilty, feeding upon those humans which he deemed culpable. The guilty were a pleasure to feed upon and Hubert found no dread or guilt when he was done with them.

Most vampires were evil and brash about killing, but realizing what they were he held no true discontent for them. The same was true for all manner of life, including the hunters.

Hunters, human for the most part, were out to defend humanity and cleanse the Earth of its evil. They were doing a job when they killed Martyre. Hubert held no ill will for the hunters and sought no vengeance. Life was about choices and how one lived with them. Martyre had said, "If cattle could carry guns there'd be a lot less hamburgers for dinner." Hubert had agreed.

One evening while chasing a woman, (who by the way had killed her husband for money while she screwed his best friend behind his back) Hubert was captured by a group of hunters, the McAffrey brothers.

"Well, well, what do we have here, boys?" The biggest of the three said. The man was standing over Hubert with a large wooden baseball bat lined with carpenter nails. Each one coated with garlic as Hubert's burning wounds attested.

"Looks like a vampire dork, Jebb," another said. (Jebb was the big one as Hubert had come to know him). The two smaller men wore large steel crosses around their necks. The crosses were blessed, as Hubert's head—developing a minor ache—confirmed. Most vampires had a hard time with blessed crosses—a partial weakening of the body or paralysis setting in—but Hubert simply found them annoying; headache inducing at the most.

Each man carried a steel lance shaped like a pool cue. They were thicker on one end and needle-like at the tip.

"Pin him," Jebb ordered.

The two subordinates stabbed Hubert in the upper pectoral area. The liquid garlic singed his skin like hydrochloric acid, making the stab wounds unbearable. They lifted him up and pinned him against the brick wall of the alley. Hubert, sounding like a frightened rabbit, squealed in agony.

"Widdle vamp get hurty?" The hunter on Hubert's left asked.

"Is he going to cry?" The other one added.

"Quiet," Jebb commanded.

"Gentlemen," Hubert began, wincing through the heat of garlic, "I'm afraid you've made a mistake. I'm with you. I hunt the wicked."

The men laughed wholeheartedly, one buckling over. Hubert went on to explain how he was once a lawyer, no longer practicing, but still studying cases. And that he reigned down punishment on those that escaped the system. The men kept laughing, even the big one.

"You know, boys, I think we have a harmless one on our hands. I mean, have you ever heard such a thing?"

"Yeah, a big superhero, pussy," the brother holding the lance on the right said.

"I think we can help our friend out," Jebb said before knocking Hubert out with one swing of his baseball bat.

Hubert awoke in the hunters' lair. Bright lights hammered his face, not ultra violet, but terrifying nonetheless. He was strapped down to a dentist-like chair. The three brothers stood around him, each one wearing a clear face shield, butcher's apron and rubber gloves. Jebb was holding a pair of pliers. A black curtain enveloped the area.

"Neutering time," Jebb howled. One of the brothers forced a steel mouthpiece—with an electrical cord protruding from it—over Hubert's mouth. A machine sounded from behind the curtain and the mouthpiece began to separate, forcing Hubert's mouth open.

"Good boy for opening so wide," one of the brothers said as Jebb began to pull on Hubert's teeth. One by one the brother yanked them out until none remained. Hubert's mouth was a bloody ruin of fleshy gums. The brothers were covered in vampire blood resembling art freaks that had gone insane. After the teeth, came the fingernails and toenails, plucked out one by one.

"Let's make sure there's no infection," Jebb said, before pouring liquid garlic over Hubert's wounds, causing him to howl in misery. He'd never felt such pain in his life.

"De-clawed and ready for domestication," Jebb said, proudly.

One of the brothers departed from the curtained area, returning with a twenty four pack of generic beer. He broke the cardboard seal and passed one to each brother. They all chugged one after another until the case was empty. It was like a vampire feeding frenzy, Hubert had thought. The brothers began kicking, punching, slapping and spitting on him. One of the men poured a can of beer over Hubert's face before knocking him out with a steel pipe.

Hubert awoke in a ditch by the side of a road in an industrial part of the city just as the sun was breaching the horizon. With his mouth throbbing, his fingers and toes pulsing with ache, Hubert stumbled upon a dumpster. He crawled inside, closed the lid, and remained there until nightfall.

Weak, tired and demoralized, Hubert found his way home. He went to his fridge and drank the emergency supply of blood he kept, before going to sleep.

The next evening he awoke to find that his fingernails and toenails had already begun growing in. Using his tongue, he felt his teeth had regenerated as well, except for two. Still wounded and shaken, he decided to stay in for the evening.

The next night his fingernails and toenails were back to normal, but his canines, the teeth that elongated into fangs, were still missing. Nervous, he decided to call his friend, a vamp named, Virina.

She was a sultry member of the undead. Virina was a true sex pot, still dressing as if the fifties were in style. After Martyre had passed, she'd taken Hubert on as a friend, but more out of pity than anything else.

"I was attacked by hunters a couple nights back," Hubert said into the telephone.

"You got away?" Virina asked.

Hubert was dumbfounded. "Do you think I'm calling from their place?"

"Very funny, Hube." He could hear Virina filing her nails. She was hardly paying attention to him and he knew it, but it was more than most did.

"I'm okay now; thanks for asking," Hubert said, angrily.

"Obviously Hube, or I wouldn't be talking with you, now would I? You sound funny by the way. Did they drug you?"

"No, it's my damn teeth."

"What about them?" Virina asked. Hubert could still hear the scratching sound of the nail-file.

"Bastards yanked them out. I'm still waiting for them to come back in."

The scratching sound ceased. Silence ensued before Virina finally spoke. "They took your teeth?"

"Yeah. Why? How long do they take to grow back?"

"Sweetie, Hube, darling. They don't grow back." Hubert heard her sigh. "Those heartless bastards."

"What do you mean? We're vampires. Forever living and regenerating. What happened to all that?" Hubert, if it was possible, was beginning to have a panic attack.

"Everyone knows heads and teeth don't grow back," Virina said, the nail-file working again. "They really screwed with you."

Hubert, lost in a thick fog, hung up the phone. Virina didn't call back. Soon the news of what happened to him would be everywhere. The woman was a gossip. Hubert stayed in his apartment for the next few weeks, too ashamed to leave. His peers would mock him and never leave him alone. A toothless vamp was a useless vamp. He hadn't many friends to begin with. This would surely lessen the ones he had except for Virina, who would always be available via telephone.

After two months of ordering in from Mobile Blood, Hubert decided to get implants. He was going to live for a long time and couldn't sulk for an eternity, especially alone.

He went to a vampire dentist and received fang implants, then went home feeling more like his old self.

During the time he spent locked away in his house, the one thing Hubert did continue to do was follow criminal cases. Law was his passion; had been so in life and was now so in undeath. It still fascinated him. Some vamps yearned for the things they loved when they were human, like the taste of hamburger, pizza, or Chinese food, or to experience daylight, lying on a beach or hiking through a forest. Hubert's craving was to practice law.

That evening Hubert went to a human occupied bar, The Vixon, where he knew a young hoodlum would be. Mickey Maroon, a gangster who killed a nine year old girl during a drive-by, but got off due to witness amnesia.

Hubert, sitting on a bar-stool and waiting for Mickey to show up, had been getting strange stares all night.

Finally, a young, drunk-off-his-ass, Wall Street want-to-be asked, "Dude, what's with the stupid fangs?"

Another buddy of his added, "This ain't no freak bar. Get lost, loser." They laughed with the women they were with as they walked away.

Hubert hadn't thought about it, but realized that the fangs didn't retract. He'd be fine in the vampire world, but in the human world he'd be made fun of, ridiculed, something he'd had enough of when he was human.

The next night Hubert went back to the dentist and had the

fangs removed, replaced with normal teeth. Depressed again, he went home and sulked.

Hubert hadn't been to many vampire functions and now he would attend even fewer. He'd only been to one orgy and managed to keep the same partner the whole time. Vampire hot spots, mostly blood bars, would be off the table. Without fangs he was unable to fully enjoy the ecstasy of vampire mating.

Hubert reminisced about the past, remembering when he was turned and how happy he thought his life would be. He had found a world where he could thrive and avoid human conditions like colds, broken bones, and most of all—bullies. But the vampire world was not much different than the human one. His fangless mouth would lead others to tease him. He'd already gotten a number of phone calls asking if his job came with a dental plan or if his dentures were guaranteed for life. Yes, Hubert had found that vampires and humans both shared the propensity to be cruel.

One night Virina called, explaining how she'd heard of a vampire getting his teeth yanked out before getting beheaded. A video of the grisly event had been left at the scene. The men wore black ski masks, hiding their identities. Hubert knew what they looked like. The images of the men who disfigured him were branded onto his brain. After hearing about the video, Hubert's nightmares resurfaced like a dead body washing ashore.

He remained indoors for the next two nights until Virina called him again. Two more videos of vampires losing their teeth and nails before being beheaded were found. For the first time, Virina was terrified. Hubert had never heard her so frightened, but an epidemic was breaking out in the vampire community. It was one thing if hunters hunted, as vampires drank blood, each species doing for their kind, but torture was evil. Hubert was the only one who knew the hunters' true identities.

The following evening Hubert scoured the area where he

was attacked. He searched back alleys and deserted roadways every night, patrolling the neighborhood, until he found them.

He followed the thugs, staying hidden, using the shadows, buildings, and trees for cover. They had a black cargo van, and Hubert managed to keep track of them on foot. He followed the van, seeing where each hunter lived as Jebb dropped them off.

Hubert went to one of the hunter's houses. Finding no alarms and a number of unlocked windows, he hid inside. Once the man went to sleep, Hubert woke him, only to knock him out with a thump to the head. An unarmed and unaware human was no match for a vampire. Hubert proceeded to the next hunter's house, repeating the same task—the man going down with ease.

When it was Jebb's turn to be kidnapped, Hubert worried about booby traps. To his surprise, Jebb was as careless as the others. None of them had thought to vampire-proofing their homes. He imagined himself lucky in that regard as the more serious hunters most likely took precautions.

Hubert had taken Jebb and his cohorts to an abandoned warehouse by the water. The building was tattered with graffiti, the windows all smashed out, and the roof barely intact. Worried about vagrants and miscreants interrupting him, Hubert scouted the area before unleashing his plan. For three nights he observed the warehouse along with the surrounding area. Not a single soul had showed.

All three men were tied to chairs, facing each other. The two cronies pleaded to be released, Jebb remained hard and stoic, he was no phony.

"Oh look, it's the toothless, pussy," Jebb said. Hubert smiled revealing his pearly whites, admiring the man's genuineness. Jebb was only being who he was. "That's impossible."

"Is it?" Hubert said.

"How'd you grow back your teeth?"

"You screwed up, Jebb."

"Go to hell," Jebb said, spitting in Hubert's direction, but missing. "I'll tear them out again, spawn of hellion blood."

Hubert wasn't sure if he was destined for Hell or if how he lived as a vampire would be his defining factor. Were vampires truly evil? Spawns of some hell or were they simply creatures from another dimension now living on Earth?

"I brought you all here for a reason." Hubert said. Jebb launched another spit ball in Hubert's direction, hitting his left shoe. "I don't know if vampires are evil, but the one thing I know for certain is that you, Jebb, are. And your followers, scarred and feeble beings, are defined by their choices. You three are as cruel as they come." One of the men began crying.

"Stop it!" Jebb yelled. "This pussy isn't going to kill us. He isn't even a real vampire. That's right, pussy. I know teeth don't grow back. You must have gotten implants. You're nothing but an old, dried up prune."

"On the contrary, Jebb," Hubert said, pacing slowly, circling the three men like a hawk stalking its prey. "You've taken my utensils, a physical part of me, but not who I am. You could've done your job, plain and simple, but I'm sure you've been a bully your whole life."

"Go screw yourself, vamp," Jebb said.

Hubert walked over to one of the men, held up an ice-pick and plunged it into the man's carotid artery. The skin popped, as if a tiny explosion had gone off in the man's neck. Blood gushed from the wound like water from a burst hose. Hubert lowered his mouth over the hole and consumed the blood. Jebb began howling curses and threats while the other man balled, the crotch of his jeans darkening with urine. Hubert repeated his actions with the next hunter, gulping down his warm blood before turning on a hoarse Jebb.

"You see I'm a vampire, nothing more nothing less, except for the handicap you've bestowed upon me." Hubert's eyes were crimson with blood and a wicked smirk found its way across his face.

"What do you want?" Jebb said. "I've got hunter's locations, whereabouts and hideouts. Let me go and I'll tell you everything."

Hubert noticed, like Jebb's partner, a darkening in the man's crotch area. The hunter made a tempting offer. Hubert could raise the level of respect other vampires held for him with Jebb's information.

"I could've maimed you, pulled out your eyes, and cut off your ears, but I'm not like you. I'm a vampire, doing what a vampire does. No more. No less. So I ask you Mr. Jebb, who is the evil one? You? Me?" Before Jebb could answer Hubert plunged the ice-pick into Jebb's carotid artery and drank him dry.

Word spread amongst the vampire community like a plague. Hubert became a hero and was invited to parties and made a slew of new friends (many of which he hadn't really liked on a personal level but thought better to have them then to not). Word hadn't, unfortunately for Hubert, only spread amongst the vampires. Hunters too found out about his actions and by the time the story had reached the humans' ears it had become quite exaggerated.

One night on his way home from an elaborate party, Hubert was killed by an arrow through his heart. Rumors quickly spread and no one knew for sure who did it. Some say hunters, others said it was a jealous vampire, but either way Hubert was dead.

The vampire community was saddened and mourned their hero's passing. A small retaliation broke out amongst vampire and hunter, not lasting long. For generations to come, Hubert's story became something of a legend, earning him the title: Hubert Humphrey: Vampire Extraordinaire. The details were inflated, as most legends are, but nonetheless uplifting and true.

Meat
Ryan Neil Falcone

I salivate involuntarily while stalking my unsuspecting prey through the congested city streets, senses tingling with predatory acuity as I track him from afar. I press against the fluid mass of people, moving unseen against the flow while focusing all of my attention upon my quarry. Now that the hunt has commenced, the perpetual hunger I endure feels distant, less debilitating. Soon, it will be sated—even if only for a short time.

My oblivious target talks on his cell phone, carelessly not paying attention to his surroundings. Why would he? With so many people around, he believes that he is safe…he has no reason to suspect the unspeakable danger he is in. I lick my lips in anticipation, running my tongue over both rows of jagged, serrated teeth, feeling a shiver of excitement within my belly that is distinctly different from the hunger.

I try to avoid making eye contact with anyone as I stagger down the sidewalk in pursuit, but find myself distracted by a child walking in the opposite direction with her mother. I am mildly amused by the visceral revulsion in her eyes when she perceives my true face. The horrified girl is quickly pulled along by her impatient mother, who cannot see me. Adult minds are the easiest to cloud. Before they disappear into the crowd, I snarl menacingly at the aghast child before redirecting the full measure of my attention back to the hunt.

For 200 years I have roamed the Earth, preying upon the fragile to satisfy my peculiar biological urges. Although I've come to think of myself as vampyr, my condition defies the popularly held notion of what this circumstance entails.

What the world thinks about vampyrs has been colored by fiction—influenced by the imaginative writings of Bram Stoker and glamorous depictions in Hollywood movies. Contrary to common belief, I do not sleep in a coffin. I am unable to turn into a bat, command packs of wolves to do my bidding, or control swarms of rats. I cannot fly, turn into mist, or move with superhuman speed. I am not impaired by religious icons, nor am I vulnerable to silver. I do not burst into flames when exposed to sunlight...although I willingly choose to avoid going out during the daytime as the darkness affords protection and makes it easier to hide my true form.

There is no element of sexuality to my conquests; my predation is purposeful. And in my two centuries of existence, I have never encountered another being afflicted by the same blight. I am eternal, but the consequence of immortality is monstrous — for while my sentience is everlasting, the body I inhabit is fragile...a pitiful, temporary vessel.

Vampyrism is a disease — a corruption of the body, perpetual decay. The consumption of blood nourishes me, but the sanguine infusion only delays my leprous decomposition temporarily. As my flesh rots, I am forced to replace failing tissue with healthy organs extracted from my victims. This wretched existence is a mockery of life — my current form little more than a grotesque, patchwork quilt comprised of body parts stolen from the unfortunate that I might survive.

I relinquished my soul long ago. My victims are meat; nothing more.

It is difficult for me to even recall a time when things were different...before the accursed hunger was upon me. Preoccupied by this question, I momentarily lose myself in recollection until my mind coalesces upon a specific memory from decades before when I'd last felt a flicker of the humanity I've so willingly abandoned.

Her eyes had been so very much like my beloved Isabella's — stirring emotions within me long believed extinguished. I'd taken them from her as a tribute to my love for Isabella...each pale blue eye a shimmering oasis amidst a desert of decaying flesh that caused my blackened heart to ache whenever I caught a glimpse of my reflection. But it hadn't taken long for these jewels to rot—their piercing purity obscured behind a diseased, milky film as they slowly putrefied. I replaced the useless baubles shortly thereafter, burying such frivolous nostalgia forever.

My name was Desoto. I sailed to the new world on a wooden ship after fleeing the old world, hiding in the cargo hold below deck to avoid being discovered. I'd abandoned my old life shortly after my innate impulses first began to manifest...after I'd first begun to feed. Those initial kills had been crude, arousing the mortified suspicion of my village, and I'd murdered Isabella out of desperation when she'd threatened to reveal my gruesome secret. It was in the aftermath of this unforgivable atrocity—surrounded by the blood and quivering entrails of my newly disemboweled beloved—that I finally understood what I'd become. I booked passage that very day, abandoning both our children and the pretenses of my old identity to embrace the monster within. I traveled to the new world in search of new victims to hunt. In search of new meat.

I shake my head to dispel this unwelcome recollection, banishing the memories from conscious thought. The hunger burning within my empty, depleted stomach reminds me of my purpose...of the biological imperative to feed and replenish. To endure.

Refocusing on the present, I realize that my prey is nowhere to be seen. I curse silently, fearing that he has eluded me, but these concerns dissipate when I catch sight of him amidst the bustling crowd ahead. I stuff my hands into the pockets of my shabby tunic and walk faster. The hunt resumes.

My condition has worsened in recent years, the decomposition of my stolen tissue accelerated by the presence of another virulent malady. I'm not sure which of my victims transmitted this pox to me, and in truth, it doesn't really matter. While my essence is not affected by the HIV coursing within my fetid veins, my stolen flesh is vulnerable. Organs that previously lasted for months now decay in weeks, forcing me to replace them more frequently. Worse still, my tissue gives off an unwelcome, peculiar stench, intensifying the necrotic odor of rot emanating from the deteriorating carcass I inhabit.

Perhaps this affliction is divine punishment for my barbaric organ harvesting — or mayhap just an unavoidable consequence of my scavenging. I know not. I do not believe in fate…nor do I feel remorse about the prospect of transmitting this disease to the victims who are lucky enough to survive our encounters. All that matters is the hunt. All that matter is cannibalizing the tissue that I need to survive. All that matters is the meat.

I brush past an easily distracted man walking his pitiful excuse for a dog. Clouding the man's mind takes minimal effort, but his overzealous mongrel is not so easily misled. I watch with grim impatience when the impertinent animal behaves as if rabid as I approach. Fortunately for both them, the trifling beast is leashed. The confused man drags the frenzied creature away, unable to comprehend what is vexing his rodent sized dog.

I give them wide berth and quicken my pace until I finally catch up to the man whose organs I intend to reap. Marshalling the full measure of my concentration, I cloud the unsuspecting man's mind and compel him to venture into an adjacent alley.

He staggers passively toward the back of the alley, away from the bustling activity of the street, away from prying eyes, away from anyone who might be able to help. I fall upon him behind a dumpster, feeling a primordial thrill the moment before I strike when he finally perceives my true form and recognizes that death is upon him. My desperate victim screams, grasping one of my rotting ears and twisting the diseased appendage from my head in a futile attempt to fend off my attack, but this only serves to anger me.

I tear out the man's throat to silence his cries, nourishing myself on the succulent nectar that flows from the pulsing death wound. Once engorged, I eviscerate the still twitching corpse, extricating his liver and kidneys to replace the rancid organs spoiling within me. The surgery I perform on myself is agonizing beyond measure, but I endure it knowing that it is the only way to ensure my continued survival. I commit one final act of disfiguring barbarism, harvesting his ear to replace the one he'd stolen from me.

When the gory task is completed, I stand above the carnage, staring into the face of the unfortunate victim. My fresh kill's eyes bulge outward, his face now frozen in a deathly expression of horrified pain. Were I capable of compassion, I might feel sorry for this stranger — but I know that chattel is unworthy of lament. The man was meat — nothing more.

Even so...there is something familiar about his haunted eyes. I pilfer the deceased man's wallet to make the attack seem like a robbery, but as I hold the unfamiliar piece of leather in my hand, something induces me to open it. My hands shake when I read his driver's license.

His name...Javier Desoto.

I stagger away from the corpse, reeling at this surprising discovery...disturbed by what it might mean. In my distraction, I fail to notice the policeman who has ventured up the alley to investigate the bloody aftermath of the attack I've perpetrated. I realize too late that I've dropped my guard, and that the startled lawman can see me.

His gunshot rips through my shoulder, but the pain helps to refocus my concentration. I cloud his mind and vanish into the shadows, leaving the startled officer to gape at the cannibalized carcass of my victim after I disappear from view. I flee the scene, losing myself amidst the endless current of people drifting through the city streets, but I'm unable to dispel the image of my victim's eyes — so much like my beloved Isabella's — from my mind. Is it possible? Could this victim with the name De-soto somehow be my distant progeny?

Before disappearing into the night, I discard his wallet in a garbage can and cast these useless sentimentalities into the wind, reminding myself that any connection to the man—real or imagined—is irrelevant. He was nothing more than meat.

Sarcophagus
Lori R. Lopez

The crypt was musty, dank and dim
A tomb forgotten by the living
Abandoned centuries ago
As if there could be no forgiving
The creature long enshrined within
A well-neglected box of stone
That housed a coffin out of wood
In which was more than meager bone
He lay in perfect agelessness
Upon an unlit funeral pyre
A man deceased and yet too vibrant
For the shell in his attire
Flesh intact, eyes shut, a hint
Of his complacent attitude
In the trace of smile that lingered
Oer an emblem stark and crude
A spike of wood that had been struck
Through the heathens ancient heart
Preventing his awakening
To rip more throats apart
With claw and fang unsheathed
But now his avarice restrained
The kingly menace stalked no more
His body harmless and profaned
Until I came across a cave
The entrance cleverly concealed
And discovered it a grave
A dormant vamp to be revealed
In a cold sarcophagus
I pushed aside the hefty lid

And removed the driven stake
Although I don't know why I did
Now he rules the world of night
And I stalk the day for him
To provide what his flock needs
Whilst my life is very grim
I am just a humble servant
Who committed a great crime
I will never be redeemed
My sins are piling up with time
There can be no absolution
I shall perish same as them
Too meek to break his hold on me
Though my actions I condemn
Had I never found that dreadful tomb
And never budged the top
Of the sarcophagus in which he slept
I could make this weeping stop.

Nocturnal Tendencies of Anthropical Thirst
Jason Hughes

"On smiling lips is innocent blood..."- Dax Riggs

"I can't believe it, Sir. There isn't a drop of blood. Not a drop... of blood." Officer Dimray said as he looked up at Detective Southland, staring back down at him. He stood up and they both looked down at the pale white and lifeless female as her milky eyes gazed back up at them. Her lips were blue and barely cracked opened, slightly exposing her top row of teeth.

"Have you ever seen anything like this before?" Officer Dimray asked as he scratched his head in disgusted confusion.

"No... No, never," Detective Southland replied as he bent over to take a closer look. "Look, there on her neck. There are the exit wounds."

"Or entrance," Officer Dimray replied as he began to scan the perimeter with his eyes.

"There isn't even dried blood on her neck. We have nothing." Detective Southland sighed as he straightened his posture and lit a cigarette. He took a deep breath and exhaled a cloud of smoke with another sigh of borderline hopelessness. "I'll call for some backup and tell the forensic department to bring some Luminol with the test kit. There has to be a stain left behind somewhere. Some kind of trace. This is just too fucking bizarre."

"Well, if they don't find out who did this, maybe the Coroner's autopsy report can shed some light on the matter... I sure as shit hope he can. This is probably just the dump site. She was more than likely murdered somewhere else and left here. It almost looks like someone wanted her to be found. I have a feeling, and it isn't good." Detective Southland firmly stated.

103

"What's that, Sir?" Officer Dimray asked with a glare of curious wonder.

"There will be more cases like this in the future... The near future if we don't get answers soon. I want them now. Get on that backup and forensic team call." Detective Southland said as he dropped his cigarette but and stomped on it forcefully with a twist of his shoe.

"Yes, Sir. I'm on it," Officer Dimray replied as he trotted to his patrol vehicle in a faster pace with each step. Soon, the entire area was illuminated in red and blue lights. One bright flash from a crime scene photographer's camera lit the woman's lifeless face as a black body bag was zipped shut, concealing her body. She was lifted into a black station wagon with CORONER written on the back in white capitol block lettering, and driven away to the morgue for further postmortem investigation.

"Man. That's a damn crying shame, she was so young. About nineteen, twenty wouldn't you say?" A nameless Paramedic proclaimed, as the Coroner wagon drove off into the distance. Detective Southland looked at him in silence, nodded his head, lit another cigarette and walked to his car.

The next night, Melissa Faracade went out to drink with a few friends.

"The body of twenty year old Christie Hernandez was found on the corner of sixth and London Street last night. Police are baffled as to how she was left in such condition and the method of operation of this heinous crime. Not a drop of blood was..." A reporter's dead toned voice announced as Rachael Creeks turned the channel.

"I love rock n' roll..." She started singing along with the newly blasting tune on the radio.

"Hey, I was listening to that, bitch," Melissa said as she playfully slapped Rachael's arm.

"Come on Mel... Wouldn't you rather jam out to some Jett than hear about gross stuff like that? It's... I don't know... depressing. Besides, we're gonna have a good time tonight, right?"

"Rock n' roll music gonna play all night," Melissa replied with a smile as she started to bang her head to the tune.

"That's the fuckin' spirit, sister. Right on... Rock on!"

Melissa and Rachael pulled into The Tower Inferno nightclub's packed parking lot.

"Shit, there's nowhere to freakin' park!" Rachael said as Melissa carefully looked around the parking lot.

"I guess here will have to do. It's a long walk, but who cares. We'll be too buzzed to notice when we leave here anyway," Melissa said as she pulled into one of the few empty parking spots.

"Or care. Ha," Rachael replied as she began to dig into her purse for blush, lipstick and other necessities for the good time that awaited down the stretch of parking lot and through the building's doors.

Melissa and Rachael pulled down the sun visors and did their hair and make – up in the small, square mirrors. They found their chosen look about five minutes later and exited the vehicle. As they closed the doors, an ambulance cruised by at a moderate pace with no flashing lights. It squealed a very short beep on the siren as it passed, just enough to get their attention. Melissa and Rachael looked at each other.

"Slow night, I guess," Rachael said as she shrugged her shoulders and straightened her miniskirt. A black car with tinted windows passed as the girls turned around to enter the nightclub. The vehicle, as dark as the night itself, decelerated slightly but kept going as it passed The Tower Inferno and evanesced into the murky distance.

Melissa and Rachael entered the club, paid at the door, got their hands stamped and proceeded to indulge in the mingling and controlled chaos that unfolded before their burning eyes and throbbing bodies.

The large, open spaced, two story building was swarming in

florescent lights, multicolored lasers and thick clouds of smoke. The music was loud and chest pounding as they ventured deeper into the vicinity. Once they entered the main floor, it was hard to move without bumping into an unknown bystander. Most were dressed in black clothing.

"I want a drink. Are you coming?" Melissa said to Rachael as she began to turn towards the bar.

"I'm right behind ya, girl. Keep movin' that way," Rachael replied as she followed close behind. The two girls were in their environment. Their surroundings were very familiar to them, although it was a place they had never been.

"What's you fine, young women's poison... or passion... for tonight?" The Bartender asked with a smile.

"I'll have ummm...Vodka...straight and on the rocks." Rachael said with a slight hesitation.

"Vodka straight... and on the rocks," the Bartender repeated with confirmation. "And for you, miss?" He continued as he looked at Melissa, with a slow up and down dip of his head.

"Bourbon. Straight." Melissa replied in a bit swifter response than Rachael.

"Bourbon straight and Vodka on the rocks...coming right up," the Bartender said as he turned and started whipping up the single ingredient drinks. He turned back around and slid the glasses to the girls with a smile. "Tonight's 'Ladies' Night'. The first three drinks are on the house, courtesy of yours truly," he said as he smiled and began to help the fellow sitting at the bar.

Melissa and Rachael got hammered pretty quickly. Their first drinks were savagely gulped within five minutes flat. Soon after, another was ordered and another... and another. Two at a time and always with exact simultaneous precision.

The man in the seat next to them could not keep his eyes from helplessly drifting in their direction. His mind had been wondering with imagination the entire time they stood next to him at the bar. "Can I get you ladies another drink?" He asked as he spun around on his stool and faced them.

"Uh... Yeah, I guess. Melissa?" Rachael said as she looked at Melissa, who could barely stand up straight.

"Um, I... I've had... I don't know..." She replied.

"Well, I'll have another..."

"I know, Bourbon for you and Vodka on the rocks for your lovely friend," the man said in a snap.

"Uh, yeah. How did you know that? Have you been here the entire time or something?" Rachael asked with a giggle.

"I have. You just haven't noticed me sitting here," he replied. The way I've noticed you two dolls, he added in a silently whispered mental note.

"Rachael, I don't feel too hot," Melissa said as she began to sway back and forth.

The way you feel is certainly far from the way you look, the man thought to himself.

"I'm going to go sit in the car for a few minutes... Maybe for the rest of the night," Melissa added.

"Are you ready to go? Ya want me to come with ya?" Rachael asked.

"No, I can manage to get myself out there. I'm just a little tipsy that's all. I'll be fine. Go ahead and have fun. I'll see you when you're done. You may have to wake me... and drive us home."

"Okay. I'll be out in a little bit. I'm just going to finish this up. I don't want to waste... his money. I'll probably have the rest of yours too. 'Kay?"

"Okay, I'll see you in a little while," Melissa said as she turned and swerved her way through the crowd and through the exit.

"Man, she is blasted toast," the man said as his head nodded down toward Rachael's legs.

"Yeah, we've had quite a bit to drink tonight."

"You think you girls will... need a ride home?"

"No, it's cool. I've got it. If not, we have friends that can come get us." Rachael replied as she downed the rest of her Bourbon and started on the remaining bit of Melissa's complimentary Vodka.

"Friends? Boyfriends?" The man asked with a slight stint of sarcastic letdown.

"No... just friends," Rachael replied as she began to sway to the music blasting all around her in ear soothing blankets of sound. Rachael's few minutes gradually stretched into a few hours. She did not notice the time flying as she continued to drink dance and make newly discovered acquaintances throughout the night.

Melissa lay in the backseat of her spinning car. A few knocks wrapped upon the driver's side window. A shadow cast over her as she tried to raise her head. Another knock, this time right in front of her rang louder on the back window. A woman in black was standing outside, looking in at her. "Hi, can you help me? I seem to be a little lost out here. Are you from the area?" Melissa gathered herself and sat up, unlocking the door. She hesitated for a moment, relocked the door and rolled down the window a crack, enough to hear the woman.

"Can... May I help you?" Melissa asked in an incoherently dazed slur.

"I was wondering if you could direct me to the nearest hotel in the area. I'm from out of town." Melissa rolled down the window. The passenger's side back door opened behind her as she felt the seat beneath her shift as if someone else was in the car. Before Melissa knew it, a large hand was placed over her mouth and she was pulled backwards and out of the car. As she looked down and tried to scream, a booted foot kicked her door closed. The woman gazed at her from the other side of the car with a sinister and almost seductive smile, and that was the last vision she recalled. A strange, sweet odor reeked from whatever had covered her face. She felt as if her nostril hairs were being singed with a potent chemical... It was chloroform. She enigmatically blacked out without a slight feeling of pain or recollection of what had just happened to her.

"Well, I better get going. I just realized what time it is. Melissa is probably waiting on me and pissed as shit." Rachael told the man that was practically her alcohol dispenser and was leaning against a wall at this point.

"Aww. You have to go so soon?" The man said with an over-dramatic hiss of despair.

"Yeah. I really need to... What was your name again?" Rachael asked as she stuck out her flimsy hand for a farewell shake of departure and acquaintance.

"Pete," he replied as he shook her hand. "It was very nice meeting you, Rachael. Tell Melissa I hope she gets to feeling better soon. She looked pretty blasted."

"Okay, I will. Thank you... and thanks again for the drinks. I think I'm set for the night."

"No problem, Rachael."

Rachael made her way to the front door. She said good-bye to others she had met earlier along the way. As she stumbled into the parking lot, she watched nothing but the ground below her pink high heels. She reached Melissa's car. She tried to open the front door, but it was locked. She tapped on the window and looked in the back. The car was empty. A car door opened and lightly shut behind her, proceeding with another. In her drunken state, she did not notice the paired sets of footsteps creeping closer behind her.

"Excuse me, miss?" A woman's voice said. Before Rachael could turn her head to put identification to the politely soft tone, it was too late. Her muffled scream almost instantly languished into a silenced whimper.

Melissa could barely open her eyes, much less move the aching muscles in her body. She forcefully pried her rapidly fluttering eyelids open and tried to hold her head up straight. The snapping of rubber gloves to her right almost made her jump, but she could not begin to turn her neck in that direction. She could hear voices around her, but could not tell which direction they were drifting from. She only knew one thing; they were very unfamiliar to her ears. None of which were Rachael.

"This one bleeds so easy," a female voice said from an unknown and remote location. Melissa opened her eyes as wide as they could possibly go. She looked in front of her and focused across the room. She wanted to scream, but something would not let her. Rachael began to become much clearer in her bleak vision on the other side of the room.

"I know, dear. She seems to drain better than the last few. It must be the alcohol in her system. We should have scavenged that area before. She should work wonders for your eternal beauty... Not that you're lacking of beauty already, my princess."

"Queen," the female voice replied. She started to sound more familiar to Melissa now. She knew that somewhere, at some time she had heard this voice before. The brainstorming inside of her head became a whirlpool of confusion.

"Hers, mixed with the others should do just fine. This will give us time to play with this one a little before you have to go back to work tomorrow night. We can then add her with the others."

"I can't wait... to play with her... and you, dear," the male said. Melissa could hear lips smacking as the two unknown voices kissed passionately in the dim lit room.

"I think you need a refill. My bottom lip isn't punctured the way you know I like it to be," the female said in an almost demanding, but mostly subtle tone.

"Yes, my dear. I will get to it."

"Good. I want it on the neck...and a little on my breast tonight," the female said.

110

"Mmm. My favorite spots, my lady. They truly taste the best."

"Help! Someone help me! Let me out of here! Someone... please! Let me out of here!" Melissa screamed inside, but could not utter a single word.

"Do you think we should drain her tonight? What if the alcohol wears off by tomorrow?" The faceless female asked.

"It probably will, but it will be better for you in the long run. You know that as well as I... Don't you, darling... Now, I must begin filing before our foreplay," the male proclaimed as he walked over to a table with a small kit on top. He opened the rectangular box and pulled out a metal nail filer.

Melissa's somewhat blurred vision was starting to get a little clearer than it had been. She saw the man, standing at a circular mirror, mounted to the wall. He seemed to have been brushing his teeth. With every swift stroke of what seemed like a toothbrush from a distance, Melissa could hear a scraping noise. The man stayed on one side of his mouth, and one tooth for quite some time. He then switched to the opposite side and began to scrape away at his other tooth. As he set the object back into the case, Melissa could tell that it was not a toothbrush, but a metal nail file. He licked his lips and turned to the woman. Melissa could feel useless adrenaline building up inside of her. She realized that her wrists and ankles were strapped down to a wooden table. She looked over at Rachael and gasped slightly. Rachael was connected to several bags with tubes connected to them, and leading into her arms and legs. Rachael was pale white and the bags were filling with her blood.

As Melissa turned her head to the other side of the room, she noticed two coffins lying against the wall. She was in some kind of homemade torture chamber, decorated as if it were in a nineteenth century castle. A cage hung from the middle of the ceiling. Right above where a bird would usually be perched, hung a bat, upside down, with its wings folded over its body. Spider and cob webs cluttered each obscure corner of the ceiling. In the corner next to Melissa was an old bathtub on small, curvy stilts. There were no faucets connected and the inner perimeter was stained in a dark rusty colored tint.

I've died and gone to Hell, Melissa thought to herself as tears ran down her cheeks. She noticed that there were no signs of holiness in her sight. Her hypothesis was far from the truth. She was still alive, and held captive in a hellish makeshift dungeon.

"I want to hurry up and bathe soon. I miss the feeling of being young, as Elizabeth before me," the woman said.

"You will always... be my Elizabeth, dear," the man said in a whisper.

"And you will always be my Vlad... now... are you ready to impale me?" The woman replied.

Melissa was hoping that everything she had just heard was a bad hallucination or dream, or even a nightmare. She wanted to awaken from these macabre visions very soon. She wished that at any moment, Rachael would come knocking on her car door window and wake her up, so they could go home safely. She just wanted to go home. I just want to go home, please... Let me go home, she thought to herself. She saw the man's hands. They were paler than the rest of his body. He was wearing white, flesh tight gloves.

The woman walked over to the man and kissed him. She proceeded to pick up the file and follow through with the same procedure to her teeth, one on each side. She set the file back into the box and turned, facing Melissa. The woman slowly walked up to her, licking her lips. Her incisors were sharper than the rest of the teeth in her mouth, and that any Melissa had ever seen. The woman got very close to Melissa and she started to tremble. She was piecing together everything that was presenting itself before her, and tried to deny it within her mind as much as she possibly could.

She felt the woman's tongue slither across her neck. It made her want to tense up and cringe in fear and disgust, but she could not move. Her incoherency was keeping her from budging the least bit. She felt a slight stinging prick on the side of her neck. Her nerves slightly twitched where her vein had been squeezed. Something warm began to run down the side of her neck, onto her collar bone. She knew what had happened in an instant. The woman began to suck on her, and roll her tongue around for a moment against her flesh. She backed away from Melissa and her lips and teeth were tinted crimson, some of which dripped onto her chin. Melissa could not believe her eyes or what was happening to her, but she began to feel it streaming in a descending flow... She was bleeding.

The man walked over to her and began the same nibbling on Melissa's other side, as the woman before him. They both had orally punctured Melissa's fragile skin and soon after, began to kiss each other passionately in front of her.

"I'm ready," the woman said as she began to undress. The taste of Melissa had turned them on and sickened her beyond belief. The man undressed and they began to passionately make love on the floor.

Rachael had lost her complexion. She was almost zombie like, hanging there motionless on the other side of the room. There was nothing Melissa could do and she had an uneasy feeling that she would soon be next. The bizarre and freakishly encounters that were taking place were far from over.

"Yes, harder! Give it to me, baby, harder!" The woman screamed in lustful bliss, as she was entered in loving thrusts. The man bit into her breasts and neck gently as she moaned louder. She nibbled on his neck and began to extract a divine hemorrhaging pleasure. The mysteriously grim couple was engaging in ensanguine romance. Their hearts were beating as one with as much passion as Melissa's was alone, pounding in fear.

The man stood up and approached Rachael as Melissa helplessly watched as he disconnected one of the tubed bags. He walked back over to the woman as she lay naked on the stone tiled ground and punctured the pouch with his teeth. He began to spill Rachael's blood all over his partner as she screamed, panted and howled in erotic pleasure. Melissa bared witness to her friend of almost ten years as she was used as a sexual stimulant and grotesque lubrication for the dark lovers that held her captive. A subtle beeping noise could be heard from the other side of the door.

"Shit, I'm on..."

"Not tonight, you're all mine...and they are all fucking ours," the woman said as she silenced him with a long, hard kiss. They continued on throughout the night as Melissa witnessed every second of their gruesome desire.

The sun's subtle rays beamed through the cracks through the boarded windows. The exhausted and sex tranced couple got dressed, lay inside the caskets on the side of the room, and closed the lids over them. Melissa could not escape. Her car had been examined early that morning by the authorities. Not a single trace of evidence was left behind, but her identification.

As the sky gradually grew darker outside, she knew there would be more to come. The room eventually darkened once more, and the doors to the beds of eternal rest creaked open. Melissa knew that she was about to endure more of the same macabre sights as the night before, until she joined Rachael in a numbing and bloodless death. She did not sleep a wink.

The woman stretched her arms as she exited the pine box of daylight slumber. "I need to bathe... tonight. My skin is getting rough. We have enough to fill the tub now... It's going to be so relaxing... I can't fucking wait."

"I'm calling in tonight. I need to be with you, my love. I'll go back to work tomorrow night," the man replied as he closed his coffin lid and adjusted his pupils to the room, fixing them on

Melissa. "Besides, I want to stay and have some fun with her as well... The both of you, darling. I can even help you bathe... and prepare for the cleansing of your skin. It will be so... soft and beautiful, my love, as you always are."

The woman looked into the mirror on the wall. "These bags under my eyes. They need to go away. I'm starting to look older. I will prepare for my bath... very soon. Maybe afterwards, we can have some drinks to start another night off together. Maybe a bloody... we never got your name, my pretty one..." the woman said as she turned toward Melissa.

Something inside of Melissa told her to scream as loud as she could. She felt her adrenaline picking up, and she was finally able to. "You sick bitch! You bastard! Someone let me out of here! Let me out of here! Help! I'm down here! They are going to kill me!" Melissa wailed as the man and woman laughed loudly. Melissa began to flail around, kicking her arms and legs. They would only go as far as the short straps would allow.

"Do you think anyone can hear you, my love? You're far from a single ear's reach," the woman replied to Melissa's tormented cries of anguished despair. She walked up to Melissa and kissed her lips. Melissa bit the woman's bottom lip as hard as she could. Blood began to pour from her mouth and onto her chin. The woman laughed diabolically and went dead silent. She began to lick her lips in a slow circular motion, savoring the taste. She spread the red fountain from her own mouth over her lips and teeth as if it were naturally produced lipstick.

The woman's lips were glistening crimson. Melissa's spontaneous plan of self defense had unfortunately backfired in masochistic and sadistic measures. "You...sick...fucks!" She screamed as her anger descended back into an ocean of oozing sorrow.

"Now, now, dear. It will all be over soon," the woman said as she wiped some of the blood from her chin.

"It's being around girls like you that make my love feel

young again, my pretty one. It refreshes her. That makes me very happy," the man said as he looked at the woman and they began to kiss. He licked, slurped and suckled the blood that Melissa had drawn from the woman's mouth.

They finished making out and the man walked up to Melissa. He licked the side of her face as she screamed and lashed her head in disgust. The couple began to laugh as Melissa looked up and noticed Rachael for the first time in which she was fully aware of everything around her. She began to scream in terror as the two laughed louder and louder.

The man walked closer to Melissa as the woman continued to cackle. He rubbed his nose down her bare leg. He began to suck on her ankle as he slowly bit into it, puncturing the skin. Melissa screamed bloody murder as the woman walked over to her. She took a savagely hard bite into Melissa's collar bone and pressed her teeth in deeply as the man continued to suck the drizzling blood from her ankle. Melissa shrieked in pain as she felt the man dig into her other ankle.

The woman backed away and looked into Melissa's eyes. "You... will help my external beauty stay young forever... tonight, at midnight," she said with a smile as Melissa started to feel woozy once more. She was slightly startled by the loud chime of a deep bell. It was that of a grandfather clock. The bells kept ringing, but she had lost count at around six. They chimed a total of twelve times, midnight had come. The bat in the cage that dangled from the ceiling began to rapidly flap its black wings.

The woman looked up and around with a smile from ear to ear. "The time has come. We'll save her for after my bathing. Disconnect the bags from the other one," the woman said in a soft but demanding tone.

"Yes, Madam," the man obediently replied. He did as she told him without further ado.

"Get the others as well. That should fill it up," she added.

"Yes, my lady," he replied as he sat the bags of Rachael's blood on the floor. He left the room as the woman turned to Melissa and looked her up and down in a sensual glare. A combination of her own smeared blood and Melissa's still decorated her lips and chin.

"Now... they will restore and captivate my beauty. You will contribute as well... in time," the woman said as her words fell upon dead ears. Melissa had given up all hope. She knew that she would never make it out alive. The man re-entered the room with more plastic pouches of tapped liquid life under his arms. He sat them down next to Rachael's, except for two. He walked over to the bathtub and punctured the bags with his teeth and began to drain each bag, two by two into the bathtub as the woman got undressed. When every bag was emptied and the tub was full, the woman stepped inside slowly, as if it were hot water. She began to rub the steaming blood all over her body as the man helped scrub her back. They kissed deep as she washed herself.

The woman lay back and relaxingly slathered her face and neck in the collective liquidation of many past victims, including the most recent, Rachael. Her lifeless shell lay on the table across from Melissa. The woman eventually got out of the tub as she and her dark lover continued into foreplay and lustful blood letting.

After the crimson cleansing and ancestry lovemaking, they approached Melissa as she lay motionless. They bit into each of her thighs and pressed champagne glasses against her legs. Each glass filled to the brim in reddish fluid. The couple held up their glasses and toasted. They wrapped their arms around each other's and drank what previously fueled Melissa's weakening life. The next night, the man known to his fellow co-workers as Christopher Wolverton, returned to work at the local hospital. He was an EMS driver.

He loved his job and the benefits.

Rest in Peace
Robert A. Read

I feel the deepest remorse for unleashing a vampire on the community. My only excuse is that we were students. It was intended as no more than a prank that rapidly escalated into unimaginable horror.

You will assume that, being a writer of stories designed and crafted into scaring my readers, that this is just another example of my twisted imagination. I wish it was, as I can be certain the parents of those young victims whose lives were extinguished in such tragic and terrifying circumstances will agree. My objective in recording the event on its, now, twenty-fifth anniversary, is an attempt to quell the demons haunting my dreams without stirring too deeply the tragic memories of those who were hurled into that nightmare experience.

The events I am about to divulge occurred back in the spring of 1976. Before that time, I had no belief in the existence of vampires. I assumed the stories to be based on myth; the affect of premature burial during the outbreaks of plague, and an attempt by an ignorant medical profession to understand the decomposition of a human body after death. I am still not convinced, but have since found it necessary to re-evaluate my beliefs on the possibility that the tales from Eastern Europe may be based on some truth.

I was attending university at Bath in southwest of England, sharing rooms in a house with five other students. Situated about quarter mile from the gates into Haycombe Cemetery, the house was a large, detached building of somber grey sandstone. Each floor had been converted into a self contained two bed roomed apartment primarily for student accommodation. The ground floor and basement were taken by our landlord. We called him Jerry—I have difficulty after all this time remembering his full name.

The apartment on the first floor, I shared with a guy named Tony Butler. He was bit of an egg-head, doing some sort of advanced mathematics and particle-physics courses.

Next level up was shared by two girls, Alice and Samantha. They were as alike as earth and air. Alice, I think her other name was Chandler, was short, a dumpy figure with close cropped mousey brown hair, and wearing glasses. Samantha Louise Tilley, with honey-blond shoulder length hair, was a tall and leggy sex-kitten who, as I am certain the other male residents will freely admit, we all voraciously lusted after.

Alice was into religion, either a Born-again Christian or a Jehovah's Witness, I cannot remember which, and was almost as prudish as Sam was sexy. Her name for Sam was a word play on her initials S. L. T. I was never able to understand how, with such differences in character, they could remain good friends. Both girls attended classes in art and graphic design.

On the top floor of the house were Ralph Rickets and one, Sebastian Malpasse. Sebastian was the oldest of us students. We believed he was between twenty-four and thirty. It was difficult to tell. The rest of us were teenagers, with Samantha being the youngest at seventeen. I remember Sebastian was intending to go into film production, but he was also into the occult in a big way. Not witchcraft; this was really heavy stuff. I think Alistair Crowley would have been considered a saint compared to Sebastian. He had all the equipment—knives, swords, wands, and books on magic and the Cabala; "Grimoires," he called them. One bound in faded leather looked pretty old, hand written I guessed, and in some language undecipherable to us. I do not know if he could read it, or whether it was just for show.

Sebastian was unbelievably tall of stature, but thin, and always immaculately groomed and dressed, whereas his flatmate, like the rest of us guys, had that long-haired, scruffy, student look so popular in the sixties and seventies.

Ralph was hoping to get into journalism, but he also displayed an interest in the occult, although his curiosity may have originated more from the influence of Sebastian. They frequently carried out rituals of some sort in their rooms — one could smell the incense from the front door of the house. I will never understand how Jerry seemed not to notice. They once showed me a pentagram they had drawn and painted on the floorboards beneath the carpet in their apartment. It was most impressive even though I had no understanding of its meaning.

Samantha also got involved in the rituals, again, probably due to the charisma of Sebastian. From articles I read on the subject, sex was frequently a part of the ceremonies, and this may have sparked her interest.

It was around this time that tales hit the newspaper headlines of someone being attacked by a vampire at Highgate Cemetery in North London. It is a very well documented case. I have no knowledge whether it was a real vampire or not, but it attracted the attention of a few self professed vampire hunters. One of them claimed to have discovered the undead creature's coffin in the cellar of an empty, detached house adjoining the cemetery. He dragged it out and set fire to it, after which, the vampire seemed to have been laid to rest. This also was the time when the film company, Hammer, was making the Dracula Movies with Christopher Lee, and Vampire legends were becoming very popular. I think it was for these reasons Sebastian got the notion of holding some sort of ritual in the cemetery to conjure up a demonic vampire.

The latest Hammer film The Satanic Rites of Count Dracula was showing in the cinemas in Bath. In the opening sequence, a naked girl lies on the sacrificial altar, her blood used to bring a vampyric creature back to life. Sebastian had no problem in persuading Samantha to play the part, but only after he promised her it would not involve the spilling of any blood. Ralph as Sebastian's neophyte had agreed to assist, and we were all invited to participate.

Alice, as was typical of her, would have nothing to do with the unholy scheme and did her best to talk Samantha out of any involvement. Tony and I however, although we had no real belief in the occult, leapt at the chance of seeing Sam stripped naked. To us, it was little more than a bizarre game.

A Saturday night in the first week of April, the full of the moon, was earmarked as the date for the event. The hour of 1:00 a.m. on Sunday morning seemed a likely time at which we could work in the cemetery undisturbed. Sebastian said he and Ralph would need a few hours in privacy to prepare for the ritual and under no circumstances must they be disturbed. They would join us at midnight.

As the day progressed, Samantha began to have doubts on the sanity of her intentions. Tony and I spent the hours through Saturday evening, with the aid of alcohol and a few wacky-baccy cigarettes, in combating those fears. It was only later how deeply I came to regret our over-enthusiastic persuasion.

At the appointed hour to the minute Sebastian arrived, wearing a robe of deep blue decorated with strange letters or symbols, and complete with cowled hood. Ralph was similarly attired but in plain white, and he also carried white robes for the three of us. Apparently, there is significance in the colors, blue for the master magician, white for the student. He also stated that the garment must be worn next to the skin, but early spring with expected night time temperatures of five or six Celsius, Tony and I said, "Stuff that." You can imagine how impressed we were that Samantha had agreed to take part at all.

Although the iron gates were some distance from the house, we could obtain entry into the cemetery through some loose railings almost opposite our front door. We thought it better not to draw too much attention to ourselves by walking down the main street dressed in those robes. There was still quite a lot of traffic and, being a Saturday night, police presence on the roads, even at that hour.

The cemetery was laid out in Victorian times like ornamental gardens, with tree lined paths leading between the tombs and mausoleums. One would be following a graveled walkway into a grotto of yew trees and come across another private crypt of some wealthy nineteenth century family. It can be very spooky and rather intimidating when a larger than life-sized stone angel suddenly materializes out of the darkness.

We all followed Sebastian, Ralph carrying a hold-all containing, we assumed, the occult paraphernalia, to a sepulcher in one such grotto. It was a large rectangular stone box, around seven feet long by four in width. Built onto a base that acted like a step around the four walls, it appeared solid in construction with no evidence of subsidence, a tribute to the craft of the mason. The long side we faced was sculpted with, what was probably, a floral motif, but now etched and eroded by wind and rain. The top was flat like a table with the edges finished in a crumbling, fluted cornice. I had no idea if this particular tomb carried any significance. I cannot even remember thinking of looking for a name engraved in the masonry. The thrill of helping Samantha disrobe chased such thoughts right out of my head.

We spoke in whispers not to disturb the haunting silence that hung beneath the trees. There was only the faint rustle of branches in the slight breeze; even the ever-present hum of a city that never sleeps seemed deadened. The full moon tried its hardest to part a ragged curtain of tumbling clouds. Waxing and waning silvery light intensified the moving shadows, making them appear to be cast by meandering ogres and ghouls. Other than the moon and the neon glow leaking from the city into the night sky reflected from the clouds, we would have been in darkness. The gloom, I guess, made Samantha less self-conscious about us ogling her nakedness, yet it still must have taken some nerve to strip in front of four guys.

It had rained earlier in the day; damp lichen masked the decaying stone on which she was to lie. Sebastian helped her onto the tomb, about four feet above the ground and positioned her on her back with arms crossed over her breasts. At the corners of the tomb, Ralph placed four black candles fixed in holders of a bizarre design I can only describe as Gothic. Each, cast in dull silvery metal, had the likeness of a demonic head. The candles were protected in a glass open topped cylinder to shield the flame from the wind. With the wicks of the candles lighted, the glass seemed to enhance the flickering, luminous intensity like a dim electric bulb that bathed Sam's naked form in a jaundiced glow. We could see her shivering from the cold.

Sebastian gave Ralph directions of where to lay out the remaining items. There were two long bladed knives, one with a black handle, the other white. Again, I believe, the colors are significant. The handles were carved into the form of an animal's head, possibly a dragon. The blades looked wickedly sharp, although we were not allowed to touch them. Two thin tapered wands of wood of the same two colors, he placed beside the knives. There was a long, thin bladed sword; I'm not familiar with these weapons, so am unable to divulge what sort. The final item was a metal goblet or chalice which he positioned on Sam's chest over her heart.

Ralph joined us several strides away from the resting place of the deceased, leaving Sebastian standing on the far side. He lifted into the light a cloth bag bound at the top with string. Unfastening the cord he pulled out a live, white-feathered cockerel holding it above Sam by its feet. I could see the sudden appearance of the creature had put the poor girl into a state of terror. I'm sure I would have felt the same way with a vicious, curved beak snapping at my bare flesh. I must give her credit however, for remaining where she was on the stone plinth.

Sebastian began to chant what sounded like an incantation. His voice was low, husky, and seemed to intensify the echoing silence of the grave. I was unable to make sense of the words, spoken in a language with which I was not familiar. Tony said later that it sounded like a mish-mash of Latin and French. I believe Sebastian repeated the incantation several times, many of the words sounding very familiar after the third or fourth hearing. A considerable length of time passed during the recitation through which we could see Sam becoming more and more agitated. The low temperature of the air and hardness of the stone can only have added to her discomfort.

Abruptly and without warning, the words ceased. Then in one sudden flurry of movement, Sebastian snatched one of the knives from the top of the tomb and slashed it across the neck of the cockerel. The bird began to jerk, threshing its wings as feathers flew and dark blood spewed from the gaping wound. Samantha screamed and appeared to twist away from the carnage, sending the chalice toppling from its precarious perch. Ralph, galvanized into swift action, leapt to catch it before it fell to the ground. He pressed one hand over the girl's throat to subdue her struggles while holding the goblet to catch the pouring blood. Turning, he implored us to help him restrain her.

I held her arms while Tony struggled to still her legs. Ralph's grip on her throat seemed rather excessive as her eyes rolled and spittle frothed from the corner of her mouth. He must have realized the same thing as he released her before I could say anything. She lay unmoving, yet her eyes still registered panic. Much of the blood had run into the chalice, but some was pooled on her stomach and chest. Sebastian bent over her and murmured some words in her ear. She turned to look at him showing something of a wry smile. It seemed to calm her so taking the chalice from Ralph, he suggested we let her go and return to our positions.

He no longer held the bird; it must have been dead by then. Holding the cup in both hands and raising it in obeisance toward the moon, he began a new invocation. At several points, he stopped the chant and drank from the cup. I'm not sure how much blood he swallowed. It may only have been sips, but we could see the stain drooling from his lower lip and over his chin.

By this time, I was feeling the cold. Everything was beginning to seem unreal—that sort of feeling when you have had a few glasses of wine too many and you wish you could sleep it off. Sebastian's chanting was becoming more strident, more intense. I guessed he was nearing the climax, the point at which he expected something to happen. I wished we had shown more interest to ask what he was expecting. He took a last drink of the blood, and then with one arm under her shoulders, he raised Samantha's head and pressed the goblet against her lips. I am sure she was not expecting to consume the fluid as she retched when he first tipped the cup. I felt sick just watching the disgusting incident.

He forced her to drain the entire contents before he again raised the chalice toward the moon and cried out another guttural invocation. From this point, my memory of events becomes a little confused. I heard a violent bang as if someone had struck the sepulcher with a sledge-hammer. A split appeared in the stone surface on which Samantha lay and through which blazed a vivid blue light, illuminating her body in azure glory. Wisps of smoke, condensation or dust swirled up from the cracked stone.

As the light faded and my eyes adjusted to the sudden flash, I could see two of the candles had been knocked over and extinguished. Samantha was on her feet, her arms waving in wild abandon like a dervish and she screamed like a banshee. She stooped to pluck the sword from the surface on which she stood before leaping to the ground on the far side of the tomb. From the way her sword-arm rose and fell, she appeared to be fighting someone or something. Then she moved around the stone towards us slashing and thrusting, like a naked, screaming

Amazon warrior.

My nerve evaporated. I turned and fled down the gravel path, terror lending my feet the wings of Mercury, the Greek messenger to the gods. I could hear the pounding footsteps of my companions at my shoulder, although I could not tell if there were two or three runners. In blind panic, it was only by good fortune and after several minutes sprinting like an Olympic athlete, we found the main gate illuminated in the yellow glare of street lights. I stopped, clutched the cold iron rails and doubled over, gasping and wheezing in attempt to catch my breath and calm my pounding heart. Ralph and Tony were with me, but there was no sign of Samantha or Sebastian.

With the returning comfort to my lungs, and relief that we were uninjured, the reality of the situation sent icy shivers through me. We all began speaking at once, each giving our own interpretation of events. According to Tony, there was a crash of thunder and flash of vivid white lightning that arced to the ground through the stone of the sepulcher, while Ralph was convinced a figure clad in a black cape and having eyes that shone with glaring, otherworldly light, rose up out of the grave.

As we calmed down, the arguments turned to the logic of what we should do next. Tony was all for, "…getting the hell out of the cemetery and leaving the others to find their own way back."

Ralph, being much closer to Sebastian was convinced we should go back, if nothing else, to make sure he was okay. I was undecided although I was more concerned about Samantha.

The decision was made for us by the sudden appearance of Sebastian. I was surprised, assuming Samantha's attack had been aimed at him and probably resulting in horrendous injuries, yet he seemed in excellent health. He convinced us we should return, that Samantha, finding herself alone and naked in such a creepy environment would be terrified. We had to agree that this was the rational thing to do and followed him back the way we had come.

The robe and shoes Sam had worn were still where she had discarded them, but of her, there was no sign. The sword was lying abandoned on the path, while both knives remained atop the tomb. The stone appeared to be undamaged other than traces of blood which we assumed to be from the cockerel.

Splitting up into pairs, Tony and me together, we conducted a tentative search in the surrounding area. The darkness hindered our progress, and there was no reply when we called her name. After half an hour of fruitless rummaging we decided to return home and reconvene at first light. 7:00 on a Sunday morning would give us a few hours when we could search in relative privacy and, if we changed our attire, without attracting undue attention. We left her clothing where it lay so she could see it if she returned, but took the remaining items with us. I am unsure what Sebastian's intention for the dead bird was, in fact, I have no memory of seeing it again.

We spent the entire morning searching all the tombs and crypts to which we could obtain access without finding her. The clothing lay undisturbed, so I'm sure she had not returned. Just after mid day, with the number of mourners visiting the graves of their loved ones, we had no option other than to give up the hunt and return to the house. Alice was waiting for us. She was livid that we had left Samantha, although we tried to explain that we had done all we could to locate her. Alice was all for contacting the police immediately, but we convinced her that nothing could have happened to Sam and that she had probably found somewhere to sleep off the excitement. We were not exactly honest about how intense the 'excitement' had been. Sebastian said that as Samantha had willingly participated, the police would only see the episode as a student prank that had gone too far. I was worried that they would blow it out of all proportion as some sort of devil worshipping cult.

By Monday morning, she had still not returned. I think we

were all now deeply concerned—all of us, that is, except Sebastian. He, being the oldest and someone we looked up to, persuaded us to do nothing, until far more sinister events on the Tuesday caused repercussions of shock to reverberate through the neighborhood.

Two young boys, brothers of eleven and twelve years of age had disappeared. They were heading toward home on a footpath across common ground adjoining the cemetery late on Monday evening, a ten minute walk which they never completed.

The gruesome discovery of the youngest was revealed to a woman walking her dog before work on the Tuesday. News reports gave very few of the exact details, but hearsay from those with close family ties with the woman who was traumatized by the experience describe the true horror of her find.

The boy's throat had been ripped open. His corpse had lost a large proportion of blood, far more than could be accounted for by the natural process of soaking into surrounding ground. Most people assumed his death was by the teeth and claws of some wild animal and speculated that a large feline had escaped from a circus show that had been performing a short distance away the previous week.

Alice, on hearing rumors of the wild beast, was immediately prompted into reporting Samantha's disappearance to the police in fear that something of similar nature had occurred to the girl. Even Sebastian was powerless to prevent her taking such action. We all agreed to accompany her to the police station, more to make certain of giving the same, plausible story without divulging the entire truth of the events.

We gave an account of a celebratory drinking party that had gone too far when the macabre lure of moonlight over the tombs of the deceased had drawn us into the cemetery. We were unaware, on returning to the house, that Samantha was missing until much later and then assumed she was with friends. Seeing the reported disappearance of the two boys, we were now concerned that something untoward may have occurred.

The police were able to put far greater resources into searching for Samantha than anything we could muster, but even they were unable to prevent further tragedy. An elderly man and his young granddaughter were attending the grave of his wife late on Wednesday evening when something attacked him from behind. It was from him that the story of a vampire first took form.

He claimed that as he lay on the ground, the demonic creature, hideous in form as if it had risen from a grave and still wrapped in moldering grey burial shroud, lifted the child and with long wicked fangs, sank them into her neck. He was shocked and horrified but gave a description of the repulsive specter as, from the translucency of the shroud, obviously female. Flesh on the face and arms was extremely pale, "anemic looking" was the term he used. Her finger nails were long, dark in color, but more like the talons one would see on a bird of prey.

"The eyes," the witness said, "were the most startling aspect — dark shadowy pits sunken into the skull like face. But as the head turned to survey me with its baleful glare they glowed red with an ethereal light that seemed to originate within the orbs." These are his own words which I have taken from an interview he gave a newspaper reporter some two weeks after the event. Whether it was colored by traditional concepts of vampires, I have no way of telling, although, as he said he lost consciousness and was unable to report the abduction of his granddaughter for a further three hours, I have my own opinion.

It was after midnight before he was able to raise the alarm. The police immediately set up a search, but aided only by flashlights, without success. They found Samantha on the following morning in one of the underground crypts. She was lying on the floor, dirty, disheveled and almost naked, but alive. The missing child was near to her — dead! The poor girl of five or six years of age had suffered severe lacerations about her throat and neck and almost entirely drained of blood before being dismembered and partly eaten. The blood was on Samantha's hands and mouth. You can draw your own conclusions.

The witness's comment regarding the shroud was true. Sam had forced open a coffin and removed the item from a corpse that had been in the crypt for many years. Whether the garment was her attempt at retaining a little modesty, or protection against the cold, no-one knew.

Samantha was never put on trial for the murder. Apparently, she could not, or would not, answer any questions. In fact it was claimed by the press that some trauma had robbed her of the ability to speak. She was committed to a mental hospital for the criminally insane the following July. Between August and November, Alice and I visited her four times. She never showed a sign of recognizing us. She sat in a chair in her padded cell, arms folded across her chest in a straightjacket. Silent and unmoving, she stared at a point in oblivion somewhere beyond infinity. It was as if she was just a shell, a mindless husk with no sense of awareness.

The staff claimed she had shown violent tendencies, the bruises on her face were where they had been forced to restrain her. We asked why she never showed signs of violence when we were visiting, in fact, during those visits she seemed totally lethargic to the point of being in a state of trance. The response from the orderly I questioned was to show me the scars from lacerations in his forearm which he claimed she had done with her teeth. These bouts of extreme violence, he told us, only occurred during the hours of darkness. During that time her manner was almost demonic. She could suffer no bright lights and if exposed to sunlight would scream and try to hide her face as if the rays burned her eyes.

On the last visit we made, her once golden-blond hair had been shaved and she was dressed in a surgical smock. The burns and scorch marks visible on her pale skin through rents in the smock told their own tale of brutal therapy in the form of electric shock.

We received a letter informing us of her death two weeks later. Alice attended the cremation. Her account of the proceedings was weird and a touch disturbing. She claimed that during the service, she detected minute sounds originating from the coffin, and that after it had been drawn on a conveyor into the incinerator she heard a scream that was quickly drowned out by the organist's rendition of Chopin's Nocturne.

To me, it seemed strange that her parents, being, as Samantha once told us, devout Catholics, had requested cremation. I was under the impression that they believed in the resurrection of the body on the Day of Judgment and that interment was the preferred method of dispatch for the deceased.

As for Sebastian, he vanished around a week after performing the ritual. We returned from classes one evening to discover he had packed all his belongings and vacated his rooms. Ralph and I spent almost a year trying to locate him without success. We felt that as a perpetrator of those horrors to Samantha, he should be made to face some kind of retribution. I assure you I would still feel the same way if I met him today.

Wherever Samantha is now, I can only hope she is at peace and can find the charity in her soul to forgive us for the apathy we showed that spring night in Haycombe Cemetery.

Out of the Mist
John Irvine

With neither grace nor sophistication
Bèluge took the boy by one slender wrist,
nought of subtlety nor snide flirtation,
and dragged him hungrily into the mist.
He flung the child against a filthy wall,
knelt by him in the stinking refuse there,
gripped the head and held it tight in his thrall.
With a grim smile he laid his canines bare.
Moon in full regalia flashed a streak
of silver light which struck the luckless youth
full in the face as Bèluge sank his teeth
to drink his fill, and consecrate his truth.
Bèluge, blissed, failed to see the wolf emerge,
tear out his throat and howl a sated dirge.

Thy Kingdom Come
Nathan Robinson

Professor Charles Gordon quivered with excitement as the dust plume cleared. Most of the rising figures around him were coughing with the influx of particles that had been breathed into their work tired lungs; but he breathed it all in. Whatever that rocky throat coughed out at him, be it fire or flaming rocks, he didn't mind. The glory would be worth the risk of contracting emphysema later in life.

His father before him had been an explorer, starting out as a student assisting Howard Carter in his excavations of various Egyptian tombs. With such an illustrious career to follow up, Charles Gordon naturally followed in his father's footsteps into archaeology. Now it had brought him here; to this unopened tomb in Israel's Negev Desert. The excitement he showed physically didn't even compare to the fantastic tingling sensation he felt in his gut.

A young female researcher approached, he recalled her name to be Lorrie, a pretty little thing that didn't make the best of efforts to make herself more beautiful. Lorrie removed her glasses and wiped away the dust that had accumulated from the days most recent explosion.

"Professor Gordon, are you really planning on venturing into the tomb? It's late, I think many of the team would like to get back to camp in order to get some rest, we've been working for ten days solid." Lorrie blinked remaining flecks of dust from her eyes and replaced her glasses, magnifying her big, bright eyes, "A lot of the folks here were expecting to be home a week ago."

Professor Gordon looked over Lorrie's shoulder at the various figures that stood like charcoal ghosts in the yellow cloud he had created, blanketing out the vast Israeli horizon that made up the dust bowl that was Ramon's Crater. Various local guides and porters wheeled barrows brimming with rocks and soil into a large pile, several student researchers from the university stood patiently with shovels and trowels, a small squad of soldiers that the government had provided as protection in this volatile land leant lazily on the jeeps, confident that their presence alone would deter any foe brave enough to venture within a mile of the dig. Every member of the team either coughed or batted out dust particles from their hair and clothes.

"My dear, I've been searching my entire life for what ever waits inside that cave, don't you think that it can't even wait another second?"

"I think it can Professor, I think the majority of the staff would prefer to explore in the morning, when it's daylight. Possibly maybe even the day after. We all need a rest."

Professor Gordon was incredulous and wide-eyed. "You expect me to wait another full day before I can venture into the cave system? When that terrific dust storm hit, I didn't wait as we carried out the excavations around the Garden Tomb did I? Nor did I hold fire when the cursed Taliban tried to halt my exploration of Calvary Hill. I've been searching for this site my entire life Lorrie. What makes you think I can wait a second longer?"

"Nothing does, it just means that we're all very tired and whatever is in that cave isn't going anywhere. You haven't slept right in days, don't you want to be nice and fresh when we find what ever waits for us in there?"

Sullen, yet still bright eyed, Charles dipped his head and smiled at the ground. "I suppose, I just feel like a child at Christmas y'know? I'm in charge, I should be the one making the decisions Lorrie, but deep down I know that your right." Charles Gordon smiled, his gray beard opened to reveal dusty teeth, tainted brown from the plumes of dust they had all been subjected to during the days excavations.

"You need a shower Professor. I'll do you a deal. I'll ask for volunteers to come to the site tomorrow, double pay and Monday off. How does that sound?"

The young American girl drove a hard bargain, but he knew she was right. His team needed rest before they even thought about venturing deeper. Even the thought of a cool shower and a comfy bed made him yearn for sleep. Lorrie was right, his endeavors could continue in the morning, he'd be refreshed and of sounder mind and body. He needed to be at the peak of his performance in order to take it all in.

"I think you're right Lorrie. I didn't realize just how tired I am. What time is it now?"

She didn't even need to check her watch. "It's gone eight. You've made us work through dinner." She cast a scornful, yet harmless gaze at him. "Again."

"Oh dear, I have lost track of time haven't I? Okay we'll resume in the morning, but I would like a team to remain behind to guard the tomb, I don't want anybody venturing inside before I do. I want to be the first."

Lorrie gave a smile, one that inspired a confidence in Charles, then returned to the throng of bodies milling about in the dust, hollering orders to pack up. Dutiful porters began packing away tools and equipment, mechanical diggers and excavators where turned off for the night. A generator coughed then died, the interrupting din still humming in their ears now relative silence prevailed. Shovels and wheelbarrows were locked away in on-site shipping containers. Today's work was done. Everybody heaved a collective sigh of relief; the heat and hard work had affected everybody in some way, now it was time for rest.

But he wasn't about to let that fact stand in the way of progress.

The sun had finished setting over the hilly yellow plains, the bumps and twists in the landscape now a darkening orange hue. The pale-eyed moon had risen in a reddening sky and Charles hadn't even realized. How many hours had they been blasting away at the rock? Fourteen? Maybe more?

Charles cast his gaze over to the dark throat hole that sat gaping on the cliff side. Nearly thirty tones of rock had been cleared by hand and machine over the course of the day's excavations. The final blast would have easily cleared the way into the main chamber, as revealed by geographical and seismic surveys. He knew it existed, just beyond the darkness, whatever treasures or knowledge would wait until dawn. His team needed rest. Hell, he needed rest, and a shower and food. His stomach growled at him for denying it sustenance for so long. Even his hands had started to shake from the stalled flow of sustenance. History was within his grasp, waiting to be plucked from the depths of time. But it would wait until morning. Good food and rest were now of the highest priority.

Professor Charles Gordon climbed into a jeep and followed his team back down the trail to their base camp. Two weary soldiers remained behind, disappointed that their evening would be spent guarding a cave system that hadn't had the eyes of man venture inside for over two thousands years.

Fed, showered and watered, the team was raring to go the next day. Dawn hadn't even broken the skyline when Professor Gordon banged the metal pot indicating that it was time to move. The porters and guides had been given the day off to let their tired muscles recover, so he had a team of four accompanying Lorrie and him back to the cave, consisting of three soldiers and his long time colleague, the brilliant if boozy, Doctor Marcus Thorp.

They took two fully fuelled Jeeps up the trail towards the excavated cave entrance, a soldier driving each of the vehicles. A brilliant, brightening azure sky devoid of any cloud sheltered them from the dying darkness of space, the sun casting burnt oranges across the derelict desertscape, took him another world away. Whatever knowledge he gathered today would be the best gift he could ever give to himself. He dozed amiably in the back of the Jeep, happily jostled about as his thoughts took him away to treasures unknown, inscriptions, details, words from a world lost by time, royal treasures hidden away from the greedy hands of the unwashed masses, buried in hard rock to be unearthed by him. Something had to be inside, the evidence pointed to the fact. The tunnel had been hand carved, each rock and boulder placed individuating in its place by an ancient hand. Seismic surveys had revealed no sign of a cave in or land-fall, the rocks had been placed there for a purpose, and today would be the day that they discovered that very reason.

Since the discovery of the carved entrance, previous tomb raiders had already taken so much of the obstruction away for them, random rocky piles dotted around the cliff face was evidence of this. But those amateurs hadn't the manpower or the technology; they didn't truly desire glory, only riches. Charles did. It had taken him a lifetime to achieve, soon immortality would be his, and he would be remembered.

"A whisky for your thoughts?" Marcus Thorpe asked from the seat across from him, he had that dumb smile plastered across his craggy, gaunt face. He'd been drinking for breakfast again, a drunk, but an all-together brilliant man.

"The past, the future…" Charles mused, "…are they not the same? And are we not cursed to repeat our same old tired mistakes?"

"Shakespeare?" Marcus queried with a quizzical eyebrow.

"No, *moi*. Here and now. I worry that we'll find nothing."

"We have to find something. Who would go to such trouble to fill in a cave such as this one? What have they to hide?"

"True, but I can't but imagine that it's just some cruel practical joke sent across from time. I fear that our ancestors long past are laughing at us from other worldly realms."

"It takes a lot of effort to set up such a prank only to never see the resulting egg on the proverbial faces."

"True, true..." Charles wanted to say more, but anticipation kept him quiet. He wanted to keep his cards close to his chest for fear of disappointment. Expect nothing and you will be rewarded forthwith with your deserved desire.

Marcus removed a hip flask from one of his pockets and took a fiery swig, he gasped and smacked his lips, savoring the burn. Charles leant forward, meaning for only he and Marcus to hear his words.

"Marcus, could we maybe keep a lid on the old drinky for the rest of today? I'd like you as clean and sober as..."

"We gotta problem..." Lorrie announced from the front seat with her typical American twang cutting through his chide. "Look, the soldiers!"

Charles swung round from his rear-facing seat and looked out the front windscreen of the jeep. The soldiers in the forward Jeep had sprung out near the entrance to the cave, weapons drawn and approaching the entrance with caution.

"Tell them they can't enter!" Charles urgently screamed, "What are they doing?" Their jeep pulled to a stop a few feet from the soldier's vehicle.

Lorrie turned round, her brow furrowed in curious concern. "The guards we left here last night. Where are they?"

Everybody got out and rushed over to the cave entrance. Professor Gordon's eyes amassed the evidence before him. A burnout campfire, empty mess tins and two U.S. Army issue rifles discarded in the dirt. The soldier's camp beds looked partly undisturbed, they had been sat on but not slept in.

The Sergeant, a short, stocky, mountain of a man named Hallis, picked up the first rifle, the Private next to him picked up the second. The second Private scoured the surrounding scenery with well-trained caution.

Sergeant Hallis checked the magazine on the discarded rifle, the Private followed suit.

"No shots fired," the concerned Sergeant said.

The Private shook a negative head, confirming the same. "No sign of a struggle. It's like they just up and left," he added. "But where?"

The Sergeant cast his gaze to the floor, following an invisible trail that only he could see, his line of sight seemed to lead to the cave entrance.

"They're in there." Hallis confirmed knowingly.

"Without their weapons?" The Private added disapprovingly, he knew better than to have his rifle anywhere but his side, ready for action.

All eyes moved towards the entrance. Silence reigned. The simple whisper of the lonely desert breezed suggested an uneasy calm to their ears.

Professor Gordon was the first to speak. "Were they not told to *not* go in? With all due respect I suggest that you reprimand your troops Sergeant Hallis!" Charles scorned.

Lorrie held a hand up to his chest, gently placing fingers on his shirt, this minor movement restrained him. "Go easy Professor Gordon."

"With all due respect Professor. I don't think they had a choice."

"Eh?"

The Sergeant pointed down to a set of vague lines in the sand, about a foot apart leading from the missing soldier's camp and into the mouth that lay agape on the cliff-side.

"They were dragged; they were either dead or unconscious. I'm guessing unconscious, as there's no sign of any blood or fire fight. Maybe they were drugged? I don't know."

"Could whoever has them washed the blood away?" Lorrie theorized.

"Possible, but we won't know for sure until we get a sniffer dog and the MP's up here. All I know is that my men are inside that cave."

"What do you propose?" Charles asked worriedly.

"Private Thomas and myself will head in as far as we can go and see if we can find trace of the missing men."

"I can't say I'm happy about you heading inside there unescorted Sergeant Hallis."

"Then what do you propose Professor? I have two missing men and that is my priority at this moment in time. Your expedition is on hold until I find my men. "

"Your job is to protect us, you are our escort…"

"Exactly," Hollis cut in, "my men are your escort, and if my men aren't here they can't escort you safely. I could very well escort you back to camp and the entire dig will be on hiatus until the military police arrive and turn over your site…."

"But…" Charles attempted to cut in.

"But, I know how much this means to you. I want to find my men. I'm praying for their sake and their families' sake that they're okay. Maybe they are just joking around, maybe they wanted to explore the cave system, disobeying my order. I assure you I want this problem solved as much as you do."

Charles sighed. "Very well, I hope you're right."

"Private Chambers will remain here with your team. Do you know how to handle a gun Professor?"

"Never had the need but I suppose…"

Hallis placed the rifle in Charles's hands. "Only fire if you have to. Chambers will show you the basics." Hallis cast his gaze to the half-cut Marcus Thorp, the expression on the Sergeant's face showed sign that he detected the booze on his breath. His vision moved on to Lorrie.

"You're American, I take it you know how to handle a gun." He didn't make it sound like a question. Hallis indicated for Private Thomas to hand over the missing soldier's rifle.

"I was raised on a ranch, been shooting since the age of three. I can probably shoot better than all your guys put together." Lorrie boasted with her winning white-toothed smile, then she relieved Private Thomas of the rifle.

"Well, let's hope that it doesn't come to that." Hallis responded glumly. The smile faded from Lorrie's face.

Without further word, Hallis led Thomas into the cave entrance. The last they saw, was them both turning on their torches vanishing into the mouth, weapons drawn and clearly preparing for the worst.

* * *

An hour passed.

Sergeant Hallis and Private Thomas hadn't come out. By now Private Chambers paced back and forth with a permanent worried expression painted across his cheeks. The first hour had passed lazily, Chambers had given the Professor a quick lesson on how to target and fire the regulation rifle and how to reload. Thankfully he stopped the lesson at full weapon maintenance. Lorrie used the free time to go over her notes from the expedition. But nothing held more concern than what awaited them inside the cave.

Marcus drank, draining the rest of the whisky from his flask, whether it was from worry or boredom, Charles Gordon didn't ask. After his lesson in good shooting, he headed over to Lorrie and nodded her over. Charles rested his rifle against a convenient rock and had a drink of water from his canteen.

"What's up Chuck?" She said in a cheery Bugs Bunny like voice, clearly an attempt to lighten the morbid mood that had settled over them all.

"What do you say to going in?" Charles eyed the entrance hungrily. He even licked his lips, contemplating, wondering.

"In there? What about Sergeant...?"

"They've obviously found something...something worth something. They want it for themselves." The Professor figured, tugging nervously on his beard, thinking. Always thinking.

"Y'reckon?"

"What else could it be?" Charles said excitedly, yet kept it hushed and hidden from Private Chambers.

"Cave in? Natural gas leak? Who knows?"

"There's only one way to find out. I'm going in. Chambers can shoot me if he wants, but it'll be murder."

Lorrie raised her hands to her face and gave an exasperated grunt then blew out a breath of concern. "You sure you want to do this?" She said from behind her hands.

His eyes caught sight of a band of silver on her ring finger they focused in on the glinting metal. "Yeah I'm sure Lorrie. I never knew you were married?"

Lorrie removed her hands from her face and looked at the silver band, so did the intrigued Professor. She looked at him, her innocent doe eyes practically melting him.

"It's a purity ring. I'm saving myself for marriage, for my one true love, if you must know."

"And who is the lucky fellow? Or lady as the case may be?"

"I'm straight, and I haven't met him yet. But I will. One day."

"It sounds delightful. It's good to see a youngster who prides their self-respect as you do, it's far more attractive when a girl won't put out as opposed to a girl who does so readily."

"You think that?" Lorrie flickered her eyes, just briefly enough for him to notice.

"Well, yes my dear. I'm an academic, I go for women's brains rather than their bodies. The brain is the sexiest organ I know of…"

"Is that what you think, or something you say to your students in order to get into their knickers?"

Partly flustered, partly turned on, Professor Gordon grinned back. "It would be unethical of me. I've never tried to get into the knickers of one of my students…as of yet. Now if one were to make a move on me, I might feel a shift in my morals," he replied cheekily then smiled, he turned his head towards Chambers.

From behind, Marcus half stumbled towards them, eyes squinting as he faced the morning sun. "What are you two chatting about? We heading back or what?"

"Chambers has the keys to our jeep. Hallis has the other set. If you want to go back, you'll have to ask one of them. Otherwise it's an eight mile hike in the sun." Lorrie answered, sweeping back a few strands of straying dark hair from her face. Professor Charles turned his attention back to Marcus.

"Well... I'm getting bored. Either we go in or go home. I'm tired of waiting for the Sergeant to materialize. I'll have a word." Marcus winked at them theatrically then sauntered over to Private Chambers. They had hushed words, and the Private shook his head. Marcus turned back, his face dour with disappointment.

"I bet I can guess what he said," Lorrie asked.

"Says we can't go anywhere until Sergeant Hallis returns. But I say we go in. He can't shoot us can he?" Charles suggested.

"I'm in." Lorrie confirmed.

"Well I don't want to miss out. I say we go for it." Marcus slapped his hands together, "I'll get the torches," and he headed for the back of the jeep.

"I'll get my camera." Lorrie shot up and followed Marcus for her equipment.

Professor Gordon stood up, cracking out the tension that had formed along his spine. He smiled into the sun, beaming back at its celestial glow. They were going in.

Within the minute, Marcus and Lorrie had their things and had joined Professor Gordon. The three of them carried on walking towards the entrance. The young Private Chambers stood between them, readying his rifle.

"I'm afraid that I'll have to ask you to sit back down Professor."

"Private, we're going in. If you want to make yourself useful I suggest that you head back to camp and bring back help..." Charles demanded, but Private Chambers interrupted.

"Sir, I recommend that you stand down." Chambers raised his rifle, he didn't aim, just lifted it slightly. He didn't want this.

"Private you can shoot us if you so wish, but it'll achieve nothing apart from a conviction of murder on your part. I am unarmed. I have witnesses. You can't kill us all young man. And I refuse to stand by while priceless artifacts are desecrated inside this tomb."

Chambers looked over at the rifle that Charles had discarded, then turned back to the trio. He visibly swallowed. He was barely eighteen, this was probably his first real mission in the field, and he didn't want bloodshed, especially not with civilians involved.

"You should take your rifle with you. There's no telling what's in there."

"I'm a man of science Private. I don't like guns."

"I can't let you go in there alone."

"Do you want to come with us?" Lorrie offered.

"If it's all the same, I'd rather stay out here."

The Professor didn't argue any more with the young soldier. "If Hallis asks, I'll say that we snuck past you."

The young Private nodded obediently, then Charles continued advancing towards the cave entrance. Lorrie, still armed with the rifle, followed close behind him, Pentax slung around her neck. Marcus meanwhile took up the rear. They each clicked on their torches as they ventured into the hungry mouth that gaped wide upon the cliff face.

"Here goes nothing," Lorrie announced.

"Here goes something," Charles corrected.

"I'd drink to that," Marcus added with a wry smile, "but I've run out."

The sunlight began to shrink to a dying circle as they ventured farther inside.

The air-cooled, bringing up goose pimples that prickled their skin; the three of them blinked repeatedly to adjust their eyes to the darkness that entombed them. It was like descending into a dream as they left the world they had known behind on the surface.

The sunlight vanished as they followed a curve in the tunnel, now they had to rely on their torches to guide them over the random scattering of rocks that littered the tunnel floor. Charles kept his torch dipped low to illuminate their path, while Lorrie and Marcus shone theirs on the walls of the narrow, sloping tunnel. This was the deepest Professor Gordon had ventured into the tunnel. The day before, the local helpers had been the only ones sent in to set small charges and blast away and clear the opposing rock and rubble that had stood firmly in his way.

"No sign of the soldiers?" Marcus asked from the back.

"Not yet," Charles replied. "We're only halfway in, the last blast was at about a hundred meters, we'll have to clear what's left of that before we can get into the main chamber. If Hallis is going to be anywhere, he'll be there."

"You hope." Lorrie said worriedly.

"Who buries something a hundred meters under ground? It must have been a great effort all that time ago." Marcus queried.

"Something valuable, that much is clear. A treasure they didn't want any one digging out. Not by…"

A white face screamed up and out of the darkness. Lorrie raised the rifle and was half a second away from pulling the trigger when the Professor knocked the barrel of the gun to one side. If it weren't for his nametag, Charles wouldn't have recognized him and he would have by now had an extra hole in his face.

"Christ, Hallis! Are you trying to get killed, where have you been?"

Hallis had been crying, sweating and glistening blood trickled freely from his nose and ears. He was a big guy, mostly muscle reinforced by body amour, but he was shaking like he'd just seen his own death.

"*Can't...change...me...*" Hallis muttered, he tried to push past the three of them, but Charles and Lorrie held him back quite easily as if the strength had been sucked from him.

"*Let...me...*" The disturbed Sergeant pleaded weakly, his quaking form trying to worm past them.

"Hallis, what happened?" Charles demanded, taking hold of his shoulders. He shook Hallis lightly, yet he wouldn't meet his gaze, all he was interested in was getting out of the tunnel. Hallis's strength increased slightly, the mess of a man pushed against them again, eager to get back to daylight. Charles could smell the sweat pouring out of the man. And the urine. And the feces.

"Hallis, just hold on a second, we can help you..." Lorrie interjected.

Hallis pushed harder against them, his strength returning, "No...no...no. We have to go...it'll be night soon, he'll be coming out. We need to get far away!" The burly Sergeant pushed once more, Charles and Lorrie fell apart, sliding down the tunnel walls as Hallis barged past them, lumbering up the passage as fast as he could to get away from whatever the hell had scared him.

"Jesus, what's got into him?" Marcus said incredulously. He shook his head and shined his torch back down the tunnel the way Hallis had come. His hand trembled slightly at what to expect. He shivered. Charles and Lorrie got back on their feet.

"Let's find out, if it's good enough to scare the Bejesus out of a meat mountain like Sergeant Hallis, then it must be worth seeing." Charles smiled grimly then resumed his trek further into the tunnel system. Nothing would stand in his way today. He had waited far too long for glory.

The atmosphere changed, it became musty and clacky in their throats. Dirty air, not just the dust, but like it hadn't been breathed in a while. It took them less than a minute to reach the last blasted wall. Huge boulders half shrouded the entrance to the chamber. After a bout of scrambling they made it over the minor obstacle and found themselves within a vast chamber, their torches didn't even reach the roof. An eerie wind hovered past their ears, indicating that the main chamber was larger than they originally imagined.

"Hey check this out." Marcus called them over, excitement tinged his voice. He was facing the curved wall near the entrance. Lorrie and Professor Gordon approached to examine his find. A small portion of the chamber wall, only about a foot square, had been polished smooth, and an inscription consisting of three-inch high letters carved into the stone.

"Latin of some sort, a deviation maybe?" Lorrie pondered. "Can you read it?" She turned to Charles. He had already deciphered it the second he clasped eyes on it.

"It's from the Bible. Peter's message I believe…"

"What's it say? My Latin's rusty, needs oiling." Marcus raised his torch and scanned the lines of bold text on the rock face.

"Old Latin, maybe older, I can get a rough translation." Charles stuck out his bottom lip as he churned the letters up in his brain, rearranging them into some kind of sensible order.

"Tell us." Lorrie asked.

He cleared his throat before speaking, and then began. "A God raised him from the dead, freeing him from the agony of death because it was impossible for death…" The Professor trailed off.

"Impossible for death what?" Lorrie urged. She shook his shoulder gently.

Charles continued, "…Impossible for death to have a hold on him. That's what it says." A shiver trickled slowly down his spine.

"Shouldn't it say *But God*? That's how I remember it from bible study." Lorrie questioned.

"It says **A God**. Not, The God or But God. A God."

"Why inscribe that there?" Lorrie questioned, "Sounds like a warning to me."

"You would be right my child." A calm, pleasing voice, both young and old spoke from the realm of darkness that threatened to engulfed them. The three of them span round, their torches had already started to weaken, the battery life fading, their view dimmed. Charles's was the brightest, he shone the light across the chamber and it met with a platform carved from the bedrock. He raised the beam, it found the top of the platform which had portions hollowed out in the shape of the letter **T**, roughly the same size of a man, with space for a head. Another slab of carved rock maybe two feet thick and six feet long lay leaning against the base, cracked in several places. A lid had been disturbed maybe from the blasting. Had they unwittingly opened some kind of sarcophagus? Charles hoped to God that nothing precious had been destroyed. Everything must be preserved.

A pair of bare feet became illuminated, elevated off of the ground; someone was sat on the rocky platform. He wore rags, old and gray with time and wear, but neatly folded around his body. Charles spied a glinting combat knife in the man's hand, Lorrie saw it too as she raised the rifle to her shoulder, a true hunters instinct. Charles raised the torch light to the stranger's face, who shielded his gaze from the beam with his hand.

"Could you not shine the light in my eyes, friend. It's been a while since I've seen the sun," the stranger asked politely, standing up to full height.

Charles dipped the beam to his chest, obeying the strangers

command without hesitation.

He could see his face now; gaunt, dark, wild hair in all directions. His features were of dark descent but his skin was as pale as the moon. He had a beard, though it looked shorter than it should have. He had a clump of hair in his other hand. He had been shaving with the knife, pulling and cutting at his scraggily beard; he just had the hair on his head to finish his makeover.

"Who are you?" Marcus asked, despite the cool of the cave, a fearful sweat flowed freely from his brow.

"I'm just a man who wanted to teach the world a different way to live. But some people wouldn't let me. They brought me here after the deal I made." The stranger waved a hand around his humble abode. "They said it would be best for everybody because of what I could do."

"What could you do?" Charles asked coolly, just as transfixed as the others.

The stranger smiled in a trusting enigmatic way. "Anything," he said. "Anything at all. How do you suppose I speak your strange Angelo dialect? I absorbed it from the warriors you sent down. My gift. I just have to meet people and I know all about them, I absorb them, I learn from them and then I can teach them more about themselves. People need to know what they are like."

"What are people like?" Lorrie asked. She calmly lowered the rifle and pointed it at the ground, seemingly trusting of the enigmatic stranger.

"Some people don't know they're good, some people don't know they're bad. I've seen it in these men's minds. Fighting a war that isn't theirs, fighting for money that doesn't belong to them. They didn't see the true light of day so I'm afraid they didn't agree. I apologize."

"What are you apologizing for?" Lorrie asked.

The enigmatic stranger pointed to the far corner, the trio of beams followed the finger and stopped upon a tangled pile of bodies. The soldiers; limbs wrapped around each other, bones broken and twisted. Three dead. Exposed skin near translucent.

When they brought their torches back over to the stranger, he had moved closer.

"I need to ask you something, the three of you. You seem like smart, reasonable people, so I need you to be honest with me. Will you join me?"

Marcus didn't wait to answer; he turned and ran, heading back up the tunnel towards the entrance, leaving Lorrie and Professor Gordon alone with the stranger.

"He won't get far," the stranger smiled again, in that knowing, pleasant way of his. "He hath partaken in spirits has he not? I see him casting himself from the trail in a covered metal cart."

"How would you know that?" Charles asked, feeling the same urgent sense to flee as Marcus just had.

"It was part of the deal I made. I have knowledge. I see people's lives end before they do. It's a reason they put me here. But it can be stopped. You must give unto me, become a follower and eternity of bliss is yours for the keeping."

"Oh," Lorrie gasped, raising her hand to her face.

"I'll tell you the truth, as I've said to many before you, unless you eat the flesh of man and drink his blood, you have no life in you."

"That's John, chapter six. How long have you been here?" Lorrie asked.

"More than years, a life, an age and more." The stranger smiled. "Another time, another place. Tell me young girl, you haven't lain with a man have you?"

"Why would you want to know that?"

"Because I can smell that you're unbroken and pure, not yet tainted by the seed of man. Come closer. Your taste will be right. Just what I need." The stranger smiled yet again, cockily this time; beckoning Lorrie closer with a thin, malnourished finger. She moved forward like it was her duty, dropping the rifle. It clattered to the rocky floor. Professor Gordon made no attempted to stop her, all this time he had been listening he had hardly moved a muscle, transfixed purely by the silkiness of the strangers words.

Lorrie stood in front of the bearded stranger. He pulled her closer and brushed the hair from off her shoulders, opened his mouth and sank his teeth into her succulent neck; and drank. A moan escaped her lips; half pain, half pleasure. Her lips quivered and her knee's shook like a giddy schoolgirl as she lovingly caressed the strangers face with the back of her palsied hand while he gorged and fed fully.

A minute or two passed, Charles stood with his face blank, hypnotized by the scene before him. The stranger pulled his bloody embrace away from Lorrie, she fell to the floor into a crumpled pile; drained, empty, used, spent. Yet still moaning in quiet orgasmic abandon, giggling quietly to herself, seemingly pleased with what had been done to her. The stranger smiled with slick pink teeth. A glistening darkness filled his beard.

"Professor, you're a smart man; you've been to many places and met many people. Do you care to join me, become a follower of my teachings?"

"I do." Charles said with an obedient nod.

The stranger stepped closer, and held his hands up to Charles's face. "You must drink my learned friend; you may well be a valuable ally in the times ahead. Drink from the wounds I suffered, that scarred me before I could complete my agreement. I suffer these for all eternity. I am cursed."

Wordlessly and with utter devotion, Charles took the hands of the stranger and began to lap cat-like at the blood that flowed endlessly from the nail holes that had punctured his palms all that time ago.

When he'd finished the stranger said gently, "Come my disciple. We have more lambs to shepherd into my flock, the whole

Nathan Robinson

world awaits my second coming..."

Deep Cover
Rob M. Miller

I'm not a faggot, but the man was beautiful. Came into the club with a magnetism only faintly approached by those numbering amongst the rich and famous, the gaudy powerful ... the enviably pretty.

Fucker was golden.

The place, The Twist, a rompous orgy-room of after-hour partiers, stood packed, with patrons from all over the socio-economic spectrum: doctors to low-grade streeters, twenty-something wannabe-somebody-someday groupies to thirty-something almost made-its, forty-something over-the-hill blown-its, and the obligatory number of power-players. The place rocked with homeboys, chicks-dicks-and-hicks, strumming their nerves and moshing, popping, thrashing, and grinding their bodies on the dance floor to every kind of techno-beat of the modern age.

The rich and poor, ugly and gorgeous. All kinds, different minds, different wants. Walmart or Armani, it didn't matter: everybody had the same shit in common: their lust, needs-and-greeds, their emptiness, and the fact they were all meat and drink.

At the door, and on the edges of the dance floor, people stopped their activities to take in the latest arrival. The Man. They were only aware of his intoxicating presence on the barest of surface levels: his stunningly good locks, fashionable clothes ... that alluring smile.

I could drink in the all of him.

Every nuance of the vibes he was putting out. I was happy and scared. After all, I'd been tracking this guy for months, and tonight was the night. All on the line. Doing the meet and greet and starting the game.

155

He turned.

Faced me.

Looked intense.

With his eyes pinning me in place, I wondered briefly if he found me beautiful, as well. Doubtful. My young ass wasn't anywhere near his league. But we were of a type.

Drinkers.

With gaze locked in, the man must've put his attractiveness into reverse — or some kind of neutral. For as he started towards me, the crowd just seemed to part, as if he were no longer visible, or unable to be consciously registered by a mortal's mere five senses, just recognized barely enough on the most primal of levels. A signal pinging from the inner ear with its clear message: Back the hell off.

Riveted, I watched him walk towards me. It was grand. I felt reminded of the past, of my different briefings, and of how right they'd all been … and at the same time, of how far below the mark they'd actually hit.

"Now listen close," one nameless man had said, "…and pay attention. You've got to be able to spot them. I doubt that it'll be hard for … well, for you afterwards, but listen anyways." The shirt, with sweaty pits and crooked tie, my presumed teacher, had sat across the table from me, cigarette dangling from an ugly, slit-lipped mouth. "Have you ever seen a kindergartner tie their shoes? Huh? Ever notice how they got to think about every little step, like they're talking themselves through the whole damn thing: 'Make a loopsie, here. Then come around with a cute crappin' half-turn … finally pulling through the opening,' and blah blah blah."

I just stared at the guy, doing my best not to count the ceiling tiles. He'd been right of course. But how could I have known at the time? Or how more-than-right the guy had actually been?

"Now, think about the way a kindergartners ties their

shoes—their awkward, unsure chubby little fingers, trying to get it right. Now, think about an adult, a teenager even, and how they just do it. Boom! And their shoes are tied. No fuss, no muss. Like it's all automatic, like flipping a switch. Which it is. We're like that."

"Like what?" I tried not letting my disinterest leak into the question, but I failed.

"Like the fucking kindergartners, you asshole. And I mean: IN. EVERY. DAMN. THING. WE. DO. Just about. At least for the older ones. Imagine a couple hundred years practice doing something like walking? Andrew Dice Clay, with that whole lighter routine of his couldn't come close to the way these biters move. They've got a grace … a way of making us look like we're all suffering from muscle spasms. HEY? You listening?"

I should've paid more attention in my classes. But that's the way hindsight always is. Too damn late. I remembered enough though. But the lessons had only scratched the surface.

Looking at the drinker in front of me, I had to admit, that muthah could walk. Almost looked like he was gliding or sliiiiding on butter. As if he really wasn't moving at all, like his center of gravity couldn't be troubled with something as bother-some as going from point A to point B. Looked as if the world was moving instead, accommodating the bastard, putting itself out, all so this dude could be wherever he wanted to be.

Just before he reached my table, I clasped my fingers to-gether and turned my head to the left, as far as I could, exposing my neck. My nerves were on edge. My carotid started pulsing with sphincter-clinching fear, but I kept my pose, feeling the man standing beside me; and then I felt it:

PAIN.

The man slowly inserted what had to have been his finger-nail into my neck, close to my Adam's-apple.

It just slid in—like inserting an ice-pick into a ball of cotton candy — zero resistance.

I held myself. This was it, the moment, the crossroads … the point where things would either go forward or I'd end up as an inkblot in the back alley.

The nail started to move, slow-but-sure. I gritted my fledgling teeth together, doing my best to remember that as I long as I was hurting like a sonuvabitch, it meant I was still a thinking unit.

My flesh parted and then re-knitted itself as the man's nail slowly traced its lesson-teaching line across my throat and up towards my right ear. I could feel my fluid starting to flow out, only to be sucked back in by my blood-jealous body.

It creeped me out.

The man moved slowly, effortlessly, his motives murky. All I knew was he didn't want me dead and gone as of yet — not with the nail moving slow enough to let me heal. Then again, perhaps he was just having a bit of sport, enjoying some play before the pounce.

Regeneration or no, having your throat slit, is one nasty, scary, and painful piece of ass-work.

"How kind of you to show. I've been waiting for it — seeing as how you've been jaunting around my preserve for the past couple of weeks." The man stopped his flesh-parting, but left his nail imbedded into me, just below the ear. I could feel the gentlest of wiggles from it.

Purposeful wiggles.

"I … I've been wanting to meet you. I've fed, but not on your ground. And even then, only what I needed."

That part was true. The man had pissed his territory out, very clearly. Anyone, least those like us, would have instantly seen that Manhattan was owned. NO TRESSPASSING ALLOWED, VIOLATERS WILL BE PUNISHED, was an inherent part of a drinker's larder.

"Yes, I know. And that has me curious. Is why your head's

still mounted." I felt the man's strength, gleaned how little of it he'd actually used on me—about as much effort as puffing out a single vapor's worth of breath—and sat thankful as I felt his nail, probably all of two inches worth, shrink back into his finger and out my neck.

"Face me."

I turned, trying not to look too happy, or too scared, and probably failing at both.

Seated, he glared at me with penetrating eyes. They were weird. I could see their color shift through the spectrum ... hazel, brown, deep blue, and even green. His pupils shifted in their size as well, from narrow cat-slits to uncanny wide-open dilation. Damn, I didn't know he—we, could do that. Man, the things I had to look forward to if I got older.

"Now, tell me WHY?"

There was no need to ask what about. I was here. At the crossroads. I'd either be successful or end up as a piece of shapeless goo. I had rehearsed countless times for just this moment. Countless times. And all for nothing. There's no way to really prepare looking into the eyes of someone like him.

"I ... want to know why myself. I ... I'm an orphan. I've been alone."

"No patron? Hmmm?" His glare x-rayed through me like I-don't-know-what. Reading my mind? Damn well hope not.

"No. I think I was taken by someone—someone feral." There. It was done. He either believed it or not. Would either jump rope with my intestines or buy the blow.

He did something else. And I didn't know what it meant.

He laughed.

Laughed and said: "An orphan. Really."

And then he laughed some more. A sinister sound. Sinister for me anyway, because it sounded like Power. A Power that could crush me like a Styrofoam cup.

Enduring the mocking chortle, I tried to match his alpha-male stare … submissively, of course.

I don't know how long we sat. Maybe a minute or so, in real-time. But in feeder-drinker time, the sands can fall differently. Hours could be had in seconds, time flowing as an uncharitable river that no man-made time-piece could ever hope to measure.

Vampire-time. You gotta love it.

"So, you obviously know enough to keep from getting gutted outright … or worse. Where have you learned?"

I could see now that I was probably in. His curiosity had won out. His ego and self-assurance, his Power, made him feel invulnerable. Not to mention the fact I was a part of the family, so to speak.

"Up and down the seaboard. In small burbs, cities, I've met others. But they didn't want to help. Not really. But sometimes I'd be given a scrap or two of advice, a few pointers." He leaned back in his chair, comfortable, tracing a whatever on the table with a short manicured right-index finger; probably the same one used on my neck. I leaned forward and grinned. Not a haughty smile, but a … a grateful one. And then I said: "Just enough to keep from getting … well, from getting gutted — or worse."

More laughter. And I knew I was in. His chuckle was of a different kind now, a construction-worker-drinking-a-brewskie-with-a-buddy-after-work kind of snort.

I'd made it. Felt so good, I could've just ripped somebody's throat open and bathed all night. Pure A-Team. Nothing like a plan coming together. I had flown up in a rickety plane, into a god-forsaken storm, and had managed a landing, one to walk away from. Yes, I'd be flying again soon, but the skies were now going to be chartable.

After all, I'd flown them before. Many times.

Working under-cover has been my job for close to two decades. That damn long, a cop gets good at his job. A cop can also get good at being pretty bad.

I don't know how long the Bureau'd known about the drinkers, but they'd sure known about me. My record had been immaculate — on paper. And there's an understanding amongst law-enforcement personnel, that when a guy works undercover, when he — or she — has to infiltrate the so-called criminal world, sometimes appearances have to be kept up: take a joint or two, fuck a few hookers, snort some snow.

But I had really gone to town.

I'd murdered, taken shit into my veins and crap up my nose to put Tony Montana to shame. And I liked it. I'd had the best of two worlds.

Paid for ratting people out, while getting to live the wild-life. Drug dealer, Murder Inc., cowboy, I'd been a part of it all.

Then an offer I couldn't refuse. Be put down like the dog I was — permanently (sometimes not even the Bureau gives a shit about the law), or get with the program.

A new kind of program.

Become a vampire, and get a 007, license to feed, to drink all I wanted, so long as they were the scum of the earth. And all I had to do was pimp out fellow vampires. Get close, gain their trust, kill them or set them up for capture.

Capture's the fun to live for. Nothing like catching an old-one and cutting him up, putting the pieces into jars, and then watching them futilely try to wiggle themselves back together. Watching the sucker's mouth beg to be put down.

A person can't blame the Bureau. R & D in this kind of business is a must. And I see nothing wrong with having a little fun at the same time. Plunking-two-birds-with-one-stone, mother liked to say.

"So, you hungry?"

I faced him, seated in my chair, making sure I didn't look too presumptuous. "Only if it's OK with you."

"Go ahead and take a sniff. Tonight's on me."

I nodded and mouthed a thank you, making sure I looked

humble. And really, I was. After all, he could've said no. Could've struck me down without a murmur in any kind of straight-up fight.

Being a vampire has some perks. We've the traditional five-senses of seeing, tasting (especially tasting), touching, hearing and smelling. But they're all amped-the-hell-up. Way up. We can see light in multiple spectrums, can hear shit that dogs only dream about, can feel day-old dried sweat stains on a counter-top, taste fear and the blackness in a person's soul, and there's no touching our sense of smell.

I took in the whole room, again, with but two quick sniffs. And it was all there. I could smell, leaking from people's pores, all the L.S.D., P.C.P. and S.H.I.T. pumping through the club's patrons. Every different type of Mary Jane T.C.P. blowing out their minds. The dried smegma in the dancers's underwear … and the juice-soaked panties on the waitress walking past our table, (not noticing us, of course).

And I could whiff what I wanted. A particular flavor of flu-id, a B positive blood-type, packaged in just the right way. Saw her through the crowd. My special eyes making transparent all the assholes standing in the way. She was perfect. The tits and ass, blood and evil-stained soul, in all the right proportions. The Bureau and I would both be happy with this one gone.

"The knockers standing forty paces behind you. Coke, Rum, and China White going through her."

"Excellent choice," the vampire said, nodding his head in a pleased mentor-like manner. "We'll pick her up and you can dine at my place. Later we'll talk and see what's to be done with you."

"Thank you," I said with happy-confidence.

The gravy-train I'd been riding through my last four suc-cesses wouldn't last forever. Eventually the drinkers would wizen up, would realize they'd been infiltrated.

Before, they'd nothing to fear. No human could really hope

to take 'em on. Except maybe a wild, mindless feral. But they were rare. I'd never met one. Perhaps the Bureau had gotten lucky, had gotten their vial of 'special-sauce' from one of them, before injecting me. They hadn't said. A need-to-know-kind-of-thing, and I didn't need to know.

In the meantime, I could have my fun. A cake, and getting to eat it, too; who could ask for more?

And all it had taken was me going undercover one last time. Crossing the dark line permanently and irrevocably, into the deepest of covers.

I looked at the blond whom I would be deliciously exsanguinating later.

Then I looked at the person, the vampire who I knew would be my friend, given a little time — a little patience. I thought briefly how he'd end up looking with his head in a jar, begging to be put down into eternity. But not for long, there would be time for that later. For now I would just go through my tried-and-true program.

I didn't care anymore if he found me beautiful. I was to me, and that was all that was important.

Donnie Brasco, eat your heart out.

Rich Blood
John Irvine

Vadim smiled grimly in the dark. It was all too easy. A smile or two, a subtle body movement, a sigh and almost any girl was his. The current subject of his attentions had full, pouty lips, shiny with pale pink lip gloss, long, gleaming blond hair and a body to die for... funny about that. She wasn't exactly the prettiest bloom in the bunch, a bit lumpy and butch, but she was young, innocent and seemed utterly entranced by him. She also smelled of blood. Rich blood.

All vamps are loners by virtue of their occupation, but Vadim had taken his choices a long way off the usual path. Biting necks and thighs was certainly cool and mega-traditional, but whilst working briefly as a medical intern in a gynecological facility, Vadim had discovered that the nutrients in menstrual blood would allow him to lead a far more 'normal' life amongst humans. He now needed to feed only once each month, which was a wicked irony, and for the rest of the time he could pursue other camouflaging hobbies. For example, he offered night classes in writing vampire fiction, and taught poetic interpretation of the great and dark Victorian poets. He was sought after in a small, tight circle as an after dinner speaker, guaranteed to create dissention and serious discussion amongst the audience. He'd laughed as he passed on his discovery to other up-market vamps.

The girl was fidgeting and fussing, wanting change, action, anything, unable to sit still for five minutes like the bulk of her generation. Vadim flashed her one of his killer smiles and she sidled around to his side of the table, sliding her hand along his thigh. He leaned forward and licked the inside of one ear, causing her to moan softly. Her musky 'moon-time' perfume set his pheromones alight.

"Shall we go, Hotlips?"

He didn't wait for an answer, rising from his chair and striding towards the door, confident she would follow. He could hear the clatter of her spiked heels behind him as he passed out into the dark street and turned towards the unlit car park, and he smirked. Her hot blood smell was almost overpowering now that she was closer to him, and he shivered with anticipation.

Opening the car door for her, he caught a glimpse of thigh as she hiked up her skirt to enter. Soon he'd be there, where he saw. Trembling now, he circled the RAV and dropped into the driver's seat. As he fumbled impatiently with the ignition key, his head was gripped and twisted toward the passenger's side. The girl opened her mouth in a predatory grin and lunged forward, taking Vadim's throat in her jaws. She proceeded in short time to tear open his neck, eat his face and gobble a few other parts of his anatomy before shoving him out of the vehicle.

Above, a scabrous moon broke free from the confinement of heavy cloud and illuminated the sad carcass of 225 year old Vadim Popescu, broken and freshly extinct. The girl, rapturous and sated, howled quietly as she drove the car out of the car park. Approaching the Interstate highway on-ramp that would take her to the next city and her next meal, she tossed her handbag out the window into the bushes. She would get another later, and at the next town collect sufficient used sanitary pads and tampons from disposal containers to attract another easy feed.

Bleeding was good, she mused.

Shroudeater
Richard H. Fay

Buried beneath gravely earth
That lay within twilight shadow
Cast by fearfully bewitched crag,
Gustav Schrat failed to find true rest.
Cursed by memories of dark deeds,
Stirred by dread desires unfulfilled,
Roused from death's eternal slumber
By elder powers strong and fell,
Grim wretch rose from untended grave
To trouble kith and kin once more.

As hag-wrought tempest blasted peak
And thunder summoned ancient gods,
Schrat squirmed restlessly in pine box.
Foul corpse opened worm-eaten eyes
Glimmering faintly with embers
Of preternatural malice.
Mouldy mouth consumed winding shroud,
Bloody fingers clawed rocky ground,
Morbidly stiff body dug free
From its musty sepulchral bed.

While grey wolves sang in alpine glen
And black hounds bayed at waning moon
That peered through dying storm cloud veil,
Schrat sought unwholesome nourishment
Drawn from remains of fellow dead
Clawed from neighbouring tumuli.
With beastly hunger barely slaked
By rotting flesh and clotted gore,

Revenant turned smouldering orbs
Toward dwellings of fresher prey.

Endowed with otherworldly traits
Of diabolic sorcery,
Schrat slipped into deep midnight murk
Under guise of lecherous dog,
Upon the wing of death's head moth,
In the likeness of mountain vole.
With loathsome reality cloaked
Fiend roamed high mead and valley vill
To bother beast and man alike
And satisfy sinister thirst.

Trembling peasant barred cottage door
'Gainst devilishly lethal night
While malignant mind spread madness,
Putrescent breath spread pestilence,
Undead wandering spread slow death.
Demon ravaged grieving widow,
Savaged cattle secured in byre,
Stalked darkly haunted countryside
Biting, gnawing, maiming, killing,
Craving ever more pulsing blood.

As monster roved evening pasture,
Lost flocks wandered unprotected.
As unclean thing assailed parish,
Frightened villains emptied village.
Few doughty souls remained behind
To become food in Schrat's fell feast,
But lone cotter solemnly vowed
To end region's nightly terror.
Armed with holy charm and strong spade

He approached desecrated ground.

Amongst chewed bones of exhumed dead,
Entwined in gnawed burial cloths,
Schrat reclined within open grave.
Dawn's break petrified bloodless limbs,
Quelled infernal diablerie,
But could not curb demonic will.
Voices cried sacrilegious words
Invoking scenes of damnation,
But sudden blow from steel-clad spade
Silenced Hell's terrible chorus.

As sunlight gilded eastern alps,
Man bound menace in hempen cords
Strengthened with rustic spell and prayer.
Brave hero dragged bloated body
Onto deserted central green.
Flint and steel struck lit dry tinder
Igniting purifying blaze.
Monstrous cadaver cursed and screamed
'Til flames reduced it to mere ash
Blowing in slightest morning breeze.

Tears of Blood
Armand Rosamilia

Chance stared at the cruel world below him and wept bloody tears. From his perch on the topmost pinnacle of the church, he could see the city bustling underneath him, people going about their lives, free from restraint.

"What life do I lead?" He wondered aloud, stroking the black tiles of the ancient roof.

He'd been a young man well before this house of God had been built, and now he could see the cracks in its facing and the deterioration that time and weather had done to it. "To live again, walk in the sun, grow old and gray and love a woman…"

He wiped thick bloody streaks from his face onto his black cloak. How long had it been since he'd seen the sun, the light spilling softly over the lake of his former home – now rot and ruin – and the chickens welcoming another beautiful day? In four hours he would bury himself into the cold dirt of his coffin and curse the demon vampire that had turned him into this… this…monster.

A stray tile fell from the roof to his left but he ignored it. He had no fear; only the sun or a wooden stake could destroy him, and he hadn't been near either in a century. Chance didn't think he even feared Death at this point in his un-life. "What was death but another long, sorrowful dance?"

"Stupid cliché."

Chance turned at the voice but he was alone on the roof. He used his extraordinary sight but there was no one else there. It was impossible for anyone to have gotten up this high. The closest window to the roof was a full twenty feet below and offered no ledge.

"Who's there?" He hissed softly, wrapping his dark cloak around him for effect. He quickly brushed his bloody eyes so he could see well.

A footfall behind brought him spinning around, cloak billowing and fangs out. He hissed a warning and lifted into the air. He was still alone on the roof.

Chance closed his eyes and sensed a presence nearby, just out of his range. His eyes snapped open and he grinned. "A worthy foe, after all these decades? Come forth and face me, vile creature, unholy demon and spawn of Hellfire."

Nothing.

He hovered for three full minutes until his leg started to cramp. He set himself down gingerly on the roof and scanned the horizon. The false dawn was closing, and he needed to go.

The laugh was in his ear and so close that he fell forward and plummeted from the roof, striking the concrete steps with such force that the bricks supporting cracked. Chance was up in a flash, swinging wildly with his manicured hands, cutting through the empty air with a swish.

He touched his lips and felt blood where he'd inadvertently bit himself with his fangs. He sighed. "What new torment is this now that forces me to strike blindly like a caged lion?"

The yard before him was empty, with normal shadows dancing under the near streetlight and in the adjacent graveyard. Chance had often come here, just before it was time to sleep, to sit and contemplate his role in this world and his long, arduous path he'd taken. Did he want to die? Really, really die? He supposed he did at times, but when he thought of the sites in Paris or the hills of Italy or the Grand Canyon or the lights of Los Angeles... he wasn't sure he wanted to give that up, nor the many women he'd met over the years and years.

"If ye be death then take me here and take me now, under the sign of the Cross in this holiest of holy grounds!" He shouted and raised his hands to the cloudy sky.

The promise of rain was met, fat drops falling from above. Chance lifted his face to the drizzle and smiled, the water tapping his fangs and sliding down his throat. "This is why I live, to taste Mother Nature in all her cruelty and glory, good and evil held in each droplet of the wet element!"

The smack to the back of his head was like a thunderbolt, and for a second, Chance thought he'd been struck. He fell to the ground and looked to the sky. The rain was steady now but no accompanying lightning and thunder. He touched the back of his head and felt a welt where he'd been struck, the area tender to the touch. He winced and pulled his hand away. "What now?" He asked and rose slowly.

Instinctively he pulled the cloak around him and hissed, but the grounds were empty save for the rain falling. He used his superior sight to check each and every tree in the area for an intruder.

His head throbbed from where he'd been smacked. He was sure of it now; he'd been punched in the head by someone or something. But who? He'd been alone in this part of the world for so long that he couldn't even remember the last of his kind that he'd seen.

Sure, he'd turned the beautiful mortal lass Kimona a decade ago, but she'd left to be with Ramon in Portugal. Chance hated Ramon and all of his follower vampires in South America. Who needed a clan of pretty people when he could be the sole pretty vampire? It was better to be alone.

Except right now.

For the first time since the turn of the last century Chance felt alone and a bit afraid. Not since the wild natives of Guam had hunted him in their jungles had he felt so close to death. He couldn't explain it, but he felt like he was being played with. Like a kitten with a shiny new toy, and he was the feline.

"I miss you," Chance whispered, the thought coming unbidden to his sharp mind. He thought about sending out a message to her but didn't want to waste the energy at this moment. He might need all of his strength, feeling a coming battle.

Chance spread his cape for effect and rose back to the roof to get a better view of his surroundings. He was relieved to see that it was empty. He needed to mentally prepare for the war ahead. Was it another vampire? Perhaps it was a new, young turn recently bitten and stupidly challenging him?

He touched the back of his head again. He could feel a twinge of pain still, but with it, anger. A growing hatred. "I relish the coming mêlée. I haven't faced an opponent of any caliber since Louis Forks of Washington tried to stake and burn me. Come and face the beast that is Chance!" He yelled from the roof.

Several lights came on a block away and he fell to the roof and covered himself with the cloak. He didn't want to be seen. He was hoping the rain, now growing in crescendo, would hide him from prying eyes.

No locals ventured out in the storm. Within a few minutes, lights were turned off and the good townspeople decided that sleep was more important than a random yelling voice in the night. The local police force was not called and only the patter of rain accompanied Chance as he stood and wiped water off of his cloak, one of seven he'd been using for the last fifteen years. He loved the feel of it against his arms and how it looked against his puffy white shirt or black high boots. The ladies also loved it, often remarking about how handsome and unique he looked, right before he seduced them with his charm (and glamouring powers) and drank a small amount of their blood.

Chance felt the red tears coming to his eyes again when he thought of those poor souls that he'd had to drink from over the years in order to sustain the evil that he had become. He'd never killed just to kill and never ravaged a body or left a pile of eviscerated remains. He preferred to take a nip of their essence and leave them feeling a bit weaker, but alive. He didn't create others like him, because he wasn't a monster, and he hated himself more and more with each feeding.

"If it is a fight you seek then meet me on the morrow in this very spot and we shall commence this brawl." Chance tried to focus and stop thinking about things that made him sad. "Bring whatever you need, weak foe, bring an army of immortal warriors if need be, but understand that you shall perish like the rest."

Five minutes later, still posing in the rain and getting no response, Chance finally thought it was time to leave and whisked away to his hidden lair.

Chance took his soaked cloak off and hung it near the door to the crypt. Tomorrow at nightfall he would need to clean up the puddle that would form there. He hated a dirty home, even if home was merely a cellar beneath an abandoned set of buildings in the railroad yard.

Forty years ago this was a thriving part of town, and the burnt-out factory across the street used to manufacture delicious cookies. Chance would purchase five-pound boxes of the mint cookies from the night watchman and leave small paper bags of the treats for the neighbor's children. He always wished that he'd had children of his own, and doted on the kids from a distance.

Of course, once the authorities had confiscated the cookies and tested them for arsenic or poison he'd been reluctantly forced to stop. Even now the thought of having to discontinue the practice stung him.

"So many bad people in this world ruin it for the good," he said and sighed, his voice carrying through the dank corridors of his home.

His regal coffin had been set behind a false wall he'd properly constructed in the northernmost corner of the complex. The trail through the basement was trapped with lethal devices he'd obtained over the years. Without thinking he stepped past the two bear traps and didn't come close to the many tripwires. Chance ducked under the thin cord that would activate the double-bladed axe suspended in the darkness above and ignored the false knob of the door before him, and the poison-tipped needle hidden beneath.

The panel slid open and the hot air assaulted him. How he hated this place sometimes, especially during rain and snow. He decided that he would get a proper hotel room the next time he was out hunting and have them procure thick black drapes on all of the windows as well as some type of bed canopy so that he could sleep all day in comfort.

"I miss wine, a good loaf of bread, the simple bliss of biting into a strawberry, and chocolate. I would give my immortal soul for one night of these pleasures." Even his carnal delights were growing old after so long, but it was the only thing that made him feel close to human.

The ritual before retiring had not changed in over a hundred years, and Chance did it without a thought: he stripped off his black boots, Argyle socks, puffy white shirt, tight leather pants, wristbands and matching jewelry, his gold loop earrings, and dressed in a simple silk robe with silver ornamentation. When he slipped his feet into his cotton slippers he smiled.

He knew he'd need to wash the blood from his clothes tomorrow night but for now he placed them neatly on the chair next to his coffin.

"Good night, sweet day. Some time in the future perhaps you will be my death, but for now our paths shan't cross." Chance opened his coffin and took in the sweet smell of the rose petals that he'd placed inside.

It happened in such a flurry that Chance didn't have time to turn fully around. He heard the two bear traps slam shut, wires being tripped and blades being released and traps being undone and smashing in the room behind him.

He felt the cold touch on the back of his throat and saw the red eyes to his left, the grip on his shoulder and neck absolute.

"Who?" Was all he managed to croak before he felt the

wooden stake sliding into his upper back, destined for his heart.

"Who or what? I am actually a vampire. You're a ridiculous cliché that is about to expire."

The vampire, not pretty, not with conscience, not worrying about love and strawberries and walking in daylight, drove the stake with relish and killed the pretender. Satisfied, he went in search of mortals to drain of their life and their blood.

The Nemesis Within
Charlotte Emma Gledson

"So...? Where the bloody hell have you been? Gallivanting with that cheap and filthy boy again, Annie?" Jemma Gray's speech was slurred, but aggression accentuated every word. She swayed as she tried to focus on her errant fourteen year old daughter.

Annie hovered just outside the living room door with a peeved expression clouding her flushed face. "I collapsed outside the school. I have a bad headache, again. Not that you'd bloody care..."

Jemma ignored her daughter's remonstrations, and flayed her arms around dismissively. "You bloody liar!"

"Honest mum! A friend helped me up and we got talking, nothing more. I'm only fifteen minutes late mum!" Annie insisted, in a weary voice. The familiar trickle of fear pricked at her skin, causing her scalp to tighten with cold as she watched her mother's face change into a mask of malice.

"I know you were with that boy again, you bitch!" Jemma shrieked, "you good for nothing pathetic excuse for a daughter...!"

"No, I swear mum, I wasn't..."

Annie detuned herself from her mother's ranting and turned her thoughts to the 'filthy boy'. Her stomach jolted as images of Dylan Curtis filled her head, his ebony hair lolling over his emerald eyes. She recalled their sexual encounters, one in particular, which had inadvertently ended abruptly with her mother's drunken intrusion, resulting in Dylan dumping her the next day via text.

'Ta for everything Annie, but I don't want you turning out like your ma, she's a total freak! – Mother like daughter? Not gonna chance it. You got great tits though lol'.

Jemma finally ended her tirade of abuse and staggered towards the sofa. She unexpectedly began to cry, her mood changing regularly like a set of traffic lights.

Annie sighed as she watched her mother dumped herself onto the settee. Feeling depressed, she walked into the centre of the living room and began to clear up the fallen magazines and crisp packets from the floor, ignoring her mother's self-centered blubberings. She tripped over bottles of wine that lay abandoned by her feet. Jemma noticed and narrowed her eyes in annoyance. One was empty; the other still contained warm claret wine. The liquid seeped into the hungry carpet, like ink pouring on blotting paper.

"You bloody idiot," Jemma panted. "Go and clean it up, and make me a sandwich whilst you're at it." Her mother's voice was still tearful yet commanding. Fear channeled through Annie's body, she may be up for another beating if she didn't do as she was told.

"Sorry mum. I'll clear it up." Running to the kitchen for a cloth, Annie suddenly clutched her head as pain returned to penetrate her brain to a higher degree. Needing to sit after a surge of nausea tossed around inside her stomach, she dragged the kitchen chair back noisily. She sat staring at the unwashed plates that littered the kitchen table.

Her voice was shaky as she slowly began to sing to herself to drown out her mother's depressive mutterings.

"I'm H. A. P. P. Y. I'm H. A. P. P. Y. I know I am I sure I am, I'm H. A. P. P.Y."

Annie quietly laughed at the irony. The familiar wave of exhaustion hit her as she placed her head into her folded arms, a crescendo of sickness churning around her gut. After a few moments she left the table and walked sluggishly to the drawer by the sink, and popped out two painkillers from the blister pack. She didn't bother with water, but instead crunched on the bitter pills in hope the pain would ease more quickly. Exhaling deeply, she looked around her. With a mass clean up facing her, and a throbbing head, Annie felt overwhelmed with misery and tiredness. To add to her sadness, she heard the sound of her mother uncorking yet another bottle of wine. The trickling liquid interrupting the quietness, filling her with a wretchedness that no one could touch.

Annie lethargically cleaned up the front room as her mother lay on the sofa watching TV, drinking. She returned to the kitchen to take the rubbish out into the garden. On opening the back door, the fresh air soothed the pain in her head to a sufferable throb, her auburn colored hair blew against her gray eyes as a light wind fluttered out. The bin liner clinked and tinkled with the empty bottles and cartons as she heaved it into the large plastic container.

Suddenly, something moved in the periphery of her vision. A figure scurried towards the compost heap. Slamming the bin lid down quickly, Annie ran towards the direction of the fleeting form. The figure stopped suddenly in its tracks, facing away from Annie.

"Hey, you? Lost something?" Annie called out. She could tell by the fragile frame that the figure must have been a young girl of similar age. The figure remained stationary, head bowed, ignoring Annie's question. She appeared to be naked.

"Hey?" Annie yelled again. As she started to approach the figure, the form slowly began to dissipate. Annie stopped in her tracks, a smell resembling burning toast filled her nostrils and a sudden chill left her shivering violently. As the shape was in the process of evaporating, it began to turn its head, leaving only stark dark hollow holes staring back at her and then, all that remained was a whisper of wind. Annie banged her palms against her temples, feeling intense pain creep across her brow.

"What? What the hell was that?" Annie whispered to herself inquiringly and stared out into the garden waiting for the figure to reappear. After nothing but the chatter of a magpie and the throb of pain within her ears, Annie made her way back to the house, the bizarre dispersing figure etched into her aching head.

Checking on her mother, Annie let out a murmur of relief when she heard her mother snoring with intoxicated snorts. Climbing the stairs, she headed for her bedroom, desperate to lie down in the hope that her headache would finally subside. Once beneath the welcoming duvet she closed her eyes. The late afternoon sunlight filtered through the closed curtains making it difficult for her to sleep, but it wasn't long before she fell into a deep and troubled slumber.

A sudden tapping dragged Annie from the folds of sleep. She raised her clammy head from the pillow as the rhythmic pounding became louder. Her wardrobe was trembling, a knocking sharp and insistent. The resonance altered, a whispering hiss accompanied the racket. Terrified, Annie heaved herself from the bed, and crept towards the rocking wardrobe. Suddenly, the movement stopped.

Reluctantly, she opened the pine door. Annie was faced with a bony figure hunched in a fetal position. It appeared to be a child. Before she could utter a word, the figure started to rock back and forth. Again, the wardrobe swayed.

"Please. Stop!" Annie begged.

The crouched figure turned from the shadows and looked up at her. Only a pair of insipid eyes stared up at her, a thin lipless mouth, curling with menace. Annie slammed the door shut with a scream. The rocking stopped. Scrunching up her eyes in disbelief, she slowly retreated until she reached her bed then, quietly but swiftly she crawled beneath the sanctuary of her duvet and shut her eyes tight.

Annie awoke from her nightmare with her disheveled mother staring down at her. Her lipstick was crudely applied, and her wispy blond bleached wig in disarray, framing her lined puffy face, resembling a clown. Jemma wobbled from one foot to another, her mouth leering with a frightening grimace.

"So, you've been sleeping on the job? So, where's my sandwich huh? You've obviously eaten yours fatty, look at the state of you. You used to be so bleedin' thin!"

Under the duvet Annie placed her hands upon her swollen abdomen. She's right, I've put on so much weight, Annie mused. Pulling her arms swiftly from out of the covers and full of exasperation, Annie answered her mother. "You were asleep mum. I have a bad headache, remember? I had to lie down. Your sandwich is in the fridge. It's covered, so don't damn well fret!"

Her mother's face darkened, her voice cold and hard. "Don't take that tone with me, do you hear?"

Annie rolled her eyes and stared up at the ceiling with a surly expression. "Sorry," she replied, sarcasm coloring her tone.

"So you fucking well should be! Anyway, I'm going out. I'm meeting Ian, won't be back till tomorrow morning. Do what the hell you like, just don't bring anyone around here like you did last time, or I'll give you a slap. Got it?"

Annie sat up, dizziness catching her off guard as she turned to her alarm clock. The neon numbers flashed 6.16pm. She faced her mother, feeling a force of pain swell inside her head like a cresting wave. "Yes, I've got it."

Jemma sniffed crudely as she turned to the door nonchalantly. "Well, get up then, you lazy bitch, and don't raid the bloody fridge," she concluded. She staggered out of the bedroom as Annie listened to her mother plod down the stairs nosily. She waited for the front door to close.

Bang.

Annie breathed a sigh of relief.

Annie's headache still pounded furiously, even after a nap. The residual memory of her dream troubled her. The hatred for her mother intensified.

Stepping out of bed, she wobbled. Closing her eyes she gained composure. Tentatively, Annie reached for the wardrobe's door handle and held her breath as she pulled it open. Only her shoeboxes, blankets and a broken electric fan lay on the wardrobe floor. Going through the clothes that hung like corpses upon the gallows, she made sure no one was hiding amongst her garments.

Relieved that it was only a dream, Annie turned from her cupboard and headed for the bathroom for more pain killers.

The headaches she had been experiencing over the last two years triggered an upsetting memory, a memory of her father who she missed so desperately.

He had died suddenly of a heart attack when she was eleven years old. The pain of losing him was the most excruciatingly emotional pain she had ever known, other than the arduous task of caring for her alcoholic abusive mother. For a reason that had always eluded her, a sense of detachment severed any tangible relationship that would have been expected between her and her mother, she had became an evil nasty alcoholic long before her father had died. Annie often wondered if this may have been a contribution to her father's sudden demise. God how she missed him.

Reaching for the bathroom medicine cabinet, something triggered her attention through the reflection. A shadowy figure sat crossed legged on the toilet seat. Abruptly, Annie turned to look behind her. Nothing. Bemused, she blinked her eyes a few times and looked to see if the image had returned. A distorted and hideous face glared back at her, with a jaw extending into a grotesque sneer. Protruding elongated canines filled the rotting mouth, its inky eyes brimmed with crimson tears.

Screaming and with a sudden vibrating sting filling her sinuses, Annie leapt back. As she did so, she stumbled into the laundry basket, falling to the floor. The image in the mirror vanished.

Getting to her feet slowly, Annie turned and looked at the mirror hesitantly, but only her own ashen face stared back at her. With gaunt mournful eyes, enhanced with dark circles, she reminded herself of an anguished victim from a black and white horror movie. She looked rough.

Plucking up courage she gingerly opened the cabinet. She grabbed the tablets and ran down the stairs, relived to be away from the mirror and bathroom.

Clutching a glass of water, Annie absently stared out from the living room window and into the street beyond. She toyed with the idea that the images she was seeing were due to the migraines and tiredness, but an unnerving instinct told her it was not…she really must go to the doctors. She put her headaches, which she had endured on and off since her father died, down to stress, which under the current circumstances were very plausible.

Cars tore past; bikes spun by. Pedestrians going about their evening business, all of them eager to return home to their peaceful sanctuary at the end of the day. A flourish of jealously and ajar of sadness passed through her. Annie continued to gaze through the living room window when she noticed a naked child standing on the pavement watching her intently from afar. The figure was encased within a foggy mist, a frothy glow radiating around her.

"What the hell do you want from me?" Annie suddenly yelled, irritated now by the persistent presence. She turned from the window and ran towards the hall, a realization dawning upon her.

Annie entered the dining room in a panic. Turning to the side dresser she picked up a photograph of herself and her father. He was embracing her under an apple tree; the picture had been taken a couple of days before he died. She studied the picture, looking into her own once hopeful eyes.

"I…It's…me…!" Annie stammered. A dry shuffling rustle coming from behind startled Annie into a paralytic fear.

"Yes, you're right…" A childish voice whispered.

Too afraid to look behind, Annie stood perfectly still, her heart hammering as hard as the pain in her head.

The voice was teasing, mocking. "You should know me Annie. I am your twin sister. We shared the same womb until you starved me to death..."

Reluctantly, Annie turned and faced the intruder. A hideous cadaverous being, surrounded within a hazy aura stood before her. Her eyes held a milky glaze covering dark hollow sockets, rimmed with wine-red shadows. Spidery gray veins were visible under a veil of pallid skin which sagged from her puny skeletal frame like a baggy jumper. The emaciated girl's hair was dry and straggly, a dirty brown in color, but balding and falling out in coarse strands. Her features were comparable to her own, though a gruesome starved carbon copy.

She approached Annie with a hateful stare. A silent scream escaped Annie's lips as the figure tried to reach out and touch her with her malnourished hands.

"I am angry. You murdered me, you know that? You took my life and fed it into your own." Her tone was casual yet cruel.

Annie stepped back, terror clawing at her innards. "I don't understand...? I never kne..." She shook in horror as she tried to comprehend what was happening, and to whom she was talking.

"Wait, let me finish..." The repugnant visitor interrupted, her tone condescending. "When you sucked the life from me fourteen years ago, I didn't 'die'. Instead, my soul entered your thriving body. I was not prepared for you to kill me!" Her voice heightened, her thin lips turned up into a craggy sneer. "So I shared your body for twelve years Annie, right until our father died."

"But...you...are...alive...? Or are you...a...ghost?" Annie's mouth was agape as she studied the stranger; her knees almost folded as her breathing become erratic.

Anger now glowed within the sister's eyes, a shade of purple clouding over the pearly orbs. "No, I am not a ghost! I am neither in one world or another. I am in purgatory, because you rejected me!"

"I...don't understand?" Annie stammered, as she back stepped slowly.

With an unwavering stare, and moving closer, the sister explained, her voice becoming calmer. "When daddy died, his death affected me as it did you. I know how it feels to die, just as daddy did. He was alone. So, I left your body to be with him. I wanted to be with him. But he rejected me... I tried returning to you, but you too rejected me. So I'm neither alive nor dead, just floating in limbo."

There was a hush in the room, only the tick of a clock could be heard.

"But I can see you. You... have a..." Annie stuttered, hesitating before she could finish her sentence. "You have a body..."

"That's why I am here!" The twin shouted suddenly, then her manner suddenly softened once more. "I need to become complete. When you were a baby, my soul was still inside your body. My spirit progressed, developed along with yours. I attached my essence into your skin, cells, muscles and the whole framework of your being. But because I separated from you after daddy died, it became impossible for me to get back inside you. You rejected me over and over. I then became this abomination Annie... You see, each time I tried to absorb myself back into you, I only managed to take tiny little pieces from you to gain any substance, and therefore I manifested into... This." She presented her revolting deficient form with an arm gesture.

"All this has been a strain on your health Annie. Every molecule, fiber, stem of your being has been strained due to my persistence. The energy it takes for you to discard me, and the small parts I have taken from you, have damaged your immune system, that's why your head hurts. The blood vessels are busting in your head, your exhaustion..." She stopped suddenly looking directly into her sister's eyes, "...Well, you are dying Annie..."

Annie gripped her temples, pain rushing through her head like a whirlwind. "NO...! NO I am not!"

The twin's mood suddenly became indulgent, her pitch lighter. "But, you can survive this... I can save you. If you can save **me**. I need something from you." The sibling paused blinking her crusty eyes and then whispered, "I need blood, or anyone's blood for that matter." She fell silent, and peered inquiringly into her sister's anxious face.

"Blood...?" Annie questioned, in a shaky reedy voice.

"Yes... blood... to keep me alive."

"So, you have been slowly killing me all this time...?"

"If you want to see it that way, yes. But you killed me Annie... So feeding me blood, surely it's the very least you can do for me sister..." The hideous vision cocked her head to one side, grinning. In spite of her overwhelming fear, Annie continued to listen to the rest of her 'sister's' plan.

"I need to have blood to rejuvenate myself, so I can be fully formed... But if I can't have yours...there is another alternative..."

Annie recoiled at the notion of her half – dead/alive sister attaching herself and draining her blood like a parasite. She was relieved there was a second option.

"What?" Annie insisted.

"Well... It's mother..." The sister stated. "Her blood would suffice, but she must be alive when I feed, but of course, she will die...eventually..."

Another quiver of fear struck Annie. Her sister continued to unravel her deplorable request.

"Once she's dead, your suffering will end, she'll not be able to hurt you any longer. Your pain in your head will lessen and you will soon feel strong again."

Annie contemplated in silence, reality seeming a distant echo, yet the sister's words made a strange kind of sense. She did not want to die or continue to live in misery with her mother.

"So are you willing? Are you able to sacrifice our mother's life to save yours and mine?"

Annie's stomach dipped, a bitter layer of bile lined her mouth. Leaving the chair, she walked towards the window, her steps labored. A sudden rush of hysteria and panic threatened Annie's consciousness. She felt she was teetering on the edge of insanity, beads of moisture bubbled upon her upper lip, her scalp tightening in a cold embrace. Still clutching the photograph of her father to her chest, Annie turned to face her revenant twin.

"I will do it. I will help you." Annie quietly announced.

"Thank you Annie," the twin responded, the skin around her lips peeling as she smiled menacingly. "You have made me very happy…"

"She's back in the morning, first thing." Annie broke the lingering silence, and an unsettling calm descending upon her.

"I know… I know everything about you; I am part of you Annie…always have been."

Annie turned to face her sister. "What is your name?"

"They named me Laura."

The abhorrent specter in front of her, suddenly no long bore a threat, no longer a fear.

The world outside continued, and the moon penetrated the gloomy skies. The street lights cast an amber glow upon the moist pavements as the drizzle trickled onto the tarmac.

Laura touched Annie's cheek. Annie felt her sister's cold needy touch, a bond was starting to form once more.

The raucous cry from the alarm clock roused Annie. Today she would save her sister…and bring an end to her and her mother's miserable existence.

Annie still harbored an excruciating headache, the fierce adrenalin pumping within her veins, making the pain worse.

Questions, doubts and fear rattled around her head like scattering marbles falling on concrete. Was she losing her mind? Had she been hallucinating and imagined everything that happened last night?

A sibilant voice came from down the hallway confirming she hadn't imagined any of it. "She's here... Remember what we planned...and don't kill her! I will do that later..."

A metallic scraping grated within Annie's ears as Jemma tried unsuccessfully to slot the key into the lock. Annie bolted down the stairs, looking a bedraggled mess after a turbulent sleep, her headache at the maximum point of pain.

Ignoring the ache, she ran into the kitchen and grabbed the screw driver from the counter that she had placed purposely the night before. Standing silently under the kitchen alcove, she watched her mother finally stagger into the hallway.

Look at the state of you. No more mother! No more of this crap ever again.

Her mother missed the coat hook as she attempted to place her vomit stained fleece onto the coat rack that hung in the lobby, her features sagging in a drunken haze. Annie squealed as she charged towards her mother, holding the blunt tool high above her head. She rammed the weapon repeatedly into her mother's face, the steel blade puncturing her eye. Jemma fell to the floor screaming in pain.

I hope I didn't kill her...

Jemma's body lay like a sack of used rags. Her wig now rumpled and soaked at her side reminding Annie of a mutilated lamb. Exhausted, Annie dropped the screw driver to the ground. Checking she still had a pulse, Annie wiped her mother's brow with her blood smeared pajama sleeve. She turned around, searching for Laura within the shadows, hoping she would appear to applaud her actions.

"See, she's not dead. She's all yours now... Laura?"

No visions, no sister.

Only a sudden surge of pain raged within Annie's head. Her body slouched, falling against her mother's body. A scarlet eye bereft of sight, gazed up at her. Annie couldn't move and an intense fear grew within her heart. The fear of impending death. The immense pain that fused within her head finally came to an abrupt end when the threatening hemorrhagic stroke finally erupted.

The frenzied attack on her mother had brought a premature ending to the sad and lonely Life of Annie Gray.

"NO! You need to live! I need that baby! You're not supposed to die YET!" The incensed voice screamed as she watched her twin sister die. Annie's body convulsed then lay lifeless at the side of her dying mother.

Jemma moved slightly, glutinous blood seeping from her gouged eye like candle wax.

Laura manifested herself. Hovering at the top of the stairs, her expression stony, she descended into the hallway. Her transparent skin cracked, hair falling out in wispy threads as she stooped and patted her mother's shoulder.

"Ahhh, Good girl. You're still alive," she hissed. "Your blood will taste good as long as life flows within it."

Jemma attempted to speak, but only a gurgle of blood and vomit spewed forth from her mouth.

"I am your daughter, or you may want to call me The Evil Twin, whichever, because I would never have been a 'goodie goodie' like her. She was so sweet, so trusting... Have you missed me?" Laura spoke with menace and spite. Her mother groaned, fingers twitching spasmodically.

"Did you know she was pregnant? Aww, I don't think you did, did you granny? But I knew…"

A soft growl emanated from her mother's destroyed lips.

Poking her sister's corpse with a bony finger, Laura spat,

191

"You are no good to me dead, bitch." She then stroked her mother's short unkempt hair. "There, there. Don't cry Mama. You know that grandchild of yours, my niece or nephew even? I don't care either way, it would have been the perfect food for me." She tilted her head back and threaded her thin brittle fingers through her shedding wiry hair, her skull evident under thin translucent skin. "By drinking her newborn's blood I would have had all the nutrients I could ever need. I would be consuming pure innocence." Her voice was shrill as she screamed, "But poor old Annie went and died on me!" She poked her sister once more, a contemptuous snarl showing serrated rotten teeth.

"Help... me... Annie... An...!" Jemma's pathetic whimpering words finally fell from her bleeding month.

Straddling her mother's body, she sniffed her mother's neck. "So, you will have to do, and that's fine by me. I may even get a bit tipsy, seeing how much you drink!" Laura laughed wickedly and clamped her mouth into the barely pulsating carotid artery.

Laura sucked nosily, as her mother's blood gushed out between the corners of her mouth. Her teeth sank deeper and deeper into the agile flesh. She feed feverishly. Color and substance soon began to bloom within her colorless veins as the nourishment flowed within her with satisfying fluidity.

A perfect transfusion.

Her mother's body began to shrivel, her body slowing desiccating like an ancient mummy. Laura's body glowed, existence thriving within every vessel of her body.

"Alive at last!" Laura screamed in-between her guzzling. "I'm alive!"

After an hours feeding, Laura was invigorated. She stood up and kicked her mother's withered husk halfheartedly and laughed.

"Thanks mummy. May I leave the table?" From the coat

hook, Laura picked up a thin beige summer jacket, most likely to have been Annie's, and wiped the blood from her smeared face and hands.

Finally regenerated and revitalized, Laura ascended the stairs aiming for her twin sister's bedroom. There she opened the wardrobe and reached out for an elasticized summer skirt. She hitched it up around her wholesome waist. Grabbing a purple crop top from a wicker chair she dressed quickly. The ensemble fitted perfectly. Finding a baseball cap and some glittery flip flops that had been cast aside under the bed, she stood in the mirror and surveyed her new image. Her twin sister's reflection stared directly back at her. Laura smiled slyly.

No one would ever know…

Laura proceeded back down the stairs. Reaching the bottom, she studied the two cadavers that lay lifeless and redundant.

"Thank you ladies for my new lease of life. It's time for me to have a wee snack. Still feeling a bit peckish, so I'm off out for a nibble. Don't wait up!" A malevolent laugh escaped from her ruby lips as she opened the front door.

She headed out into the darkness of the night. With a tantalizing excitement thrilling her, and an exuberance radiating throughout her new wholesome body, she would never relinquish the life that now flowed through her once insubstantial body.

She licked her lips…ready to beguile her unsuspecting victims.

The Solitary Man
Alan Spencer

Solitary people harbor the best blood. The Henry David Thoreau types of the world. The loners and hermits. The people who've dedicated their lives to indulging in their own personal desires and passions. Any place secluded, where solitary and anti-social people reside, Jake Manner chose as his hunting ground. This is where he walked now, traipsing about in a dense forest somewhere in Nebraska. With each stride, he inhaled the aromatic decay of dead leaves and rotting felled trees. It wouldn't be long before he reached the log cabin up ahead. Smoke exuded out its chimney. Someone was home, but he couldn't be certain if they were alone.

Closing in on that lone cabin, the vampire became the shadows, moving with the black. He neared the window on the west side to peer inside. He caught the bright square of a tall fire crackling in its brick enclosure. The other things he spied throughout the room encouraged him to slip through the side door. It was unlocked, what proved to be yet another advantage to those who believed they were alone in the deepest of niches.

It wouldn't be hard to blend in the room, the only light being from the fire. The paintings were what drew him in here. Over thirty canvases were propped on wooden stands, as if in a private gallery. Human bodies posing naked, mostly, but with an added twist to the subject matter. Women were huddled together in groups of ten, clutching each other as if wanting to delve their fingers through each other's skin, as if craving to absorb each other. In another, men and women were woven together as if they were a human tapestry, fingers and arms and heads connecting to each other in one great flesh design. Then six canvases were put together, featuring hundreds of people melting, their flesh like dripping wax, the skin spreading at their feet and pooling up to their knees. Others in the background of the same painting were bent over to delve themselves into the flesh, bathing and saturating themselves. No blood or guts in these paintings, only skin, flesh intertwined with flesh, the human spirit celebrated in liquid.

As he ogled the flesh paintings, he couldn't help but wonder whose house he'd stepped into, and what this man's fascinations were. Investigating that question, he roamed into the kitchen to come upon a modern set up. Nothing amiss. A twenty place wine rack was missing one bottle, that bottle of Merlot opened on the counter and a glass poured.

But where was the drinker?

Where is this solitary man, the vampire kept asking himself, moving on down the hall where more paintings of flesh were displayed, namely of one where a woman kept her children warm from the winter's breeze by spreading out the skin from her torso and draping it over the shivering little ones.

The bathroom was unoccupied, as was the bedroom, though he noted the shelves of hundreds of novels with bent and used spines. In the closet, a cache of adult movies stared back at him, what had to be at least two hundred titles. Yet another stash was hidden on the topmost tier of the closet, what amounted to a big box of jewel cases with DVD's marked "Posing #35" and the highest numbered he'd discovered was "Posing #973."

The vampire released a prolonged, "Hmmmmmmmm," and continued the search, slipping into the guest room and admiring the large painting of a bustling cityscape where everyone on the sidewalks were tearing their flesh off like excessive clothing, as if freeing themselves, their faces so jubilant and liberated.

"Where's all the blood?" The vampire muttered under his breath. With all the flesh tearing and undressing of dermis, not a single drop had been shed. "This is...very strange."

He'd happened upon a very interesting solitary man tonight. His standards would be changed from here on out, he believed.

Nobody had such a fetish for painting bodies and the flesh, and the crude severing of it. The air of the place was off; it was heavy when it should've been light and clean. The questionable air was edging its way into his nose, and it was coming from the basement, of all places.

Quick as light penetrates through glass, the vampire's shadow shot back into the living room of paintings, then down through the crack of the basement door. Coasting along a short set of wooden steps, he stayed under the stairwell's shadows to view the expanse of concrete. The trickling of water - no, the spraying of water could be heard. The scent of blood was robust in the air, though it came and went, the aroma merely short lived.

Then he shifted his sight to something incredible. The bright light in the center of the room was stage powerful, and it highlighted a woman standing on a wooden stool. She was naked from head to toe. Her left arm was raised as if reaching out to pick an apple off a tree. Her back was arched, and she held that pose, though he could see her muscles visibly rise and fall and quiver. The poor thing had been holding that pose for far too long. She couldn't disguise the anguish from her eyes, the constant flux of severities.

"Hold still."

"Keep still."

"If you get off that stool, you know what happens to you."

"Now pose."

A harsh voice echoed from deeper in the room, the source hidden behind that bright wall of stage light. The vampire caught the red flickering dot of a camera. The solitary man was recording the woman to add to his collection of poses.

Becoming a shadow again, he stayed against the wall, using it as a guideline, and ventured beyond the standing woman and the bright lights to the iron barred cages. Nobody was inside of them, though there was an empty plate and a plastic water container one would use for a hamster. The smell of dirty human, like baby powder over shit, repulsed him. A rubber hose hung from overhead, what the vampire assumed was used to spray out the temporary living quarters clean.

The greatest insult was still in the coming. This solitary man, the pervert, the sociopath, the overzealous monster, had a male corpse hanging up by its ankles with a hook driven through the flesh and bone. Red bullets of blood streamed down its body in tandem with the blood escaping the dead man's sliced wrists and jugular and carotid artery. And the bastard, he thought, was using a hose to spray the blood down the drain. He was wasting good blood.

The insult!

The nerve!

He pounced on the man with gray hair running down to his shoulders in greasy ropes, dressed only in jeans and a rubber apron, the solitary man in his later middle age. The man unleashed a yelp of shock as the vampire went from shadow to solid form and bit him between his deltoid and throat, sucking the crimson that bubbled to the surface. After one long drink, his mouth and chin and chest spattered in his meal, he kicked the solitary man to the ground. He would soon be paralyzed, the enzymes in his bite able to cripple a man up to three hundred pounds.

The woman remained standing on top of the stool, rigid, unmoving, and terrified out of her mind. Her ability to make decisions for herself had been stolen. She didn't perceive his touch or her removal from the pedestal. He roamed the room, locating stray articles of clothing: a pair of women's jeans, a torn midriff, a purse, and running shoes. He helped her slip back into the clothing. Her eyes were unblinking, in a trance, trapped in a dark, dark place, the place the solitary man had exiled her.

"My husband," she'd whisper from a clenched throat. "My husband...he killed...my...husband...is dead..."

The vampire, sensing what had happened, the couple taken from their lives to be submitted to tortures - and he questioned how many of those flesh paintings upstairs were from the solitary man's imagination or instead rendered from still life poses - he understood that it was her husband who was being washed off in the corner, cleaned of blood.

He breathed into her mouth, releasing a potent chemical that would turn her into an obedient zombie, temporarily. She'd hike to the road and find help. Forget she met him or the solitary man. She'd be safe, though without a husband, she had survived the terrible ordeal.

The woman was up and leaving the premises in a matter of minutes.

Then left him and solitary man.

The vampire interrogated his victim. Trying to frame a sensible question, he simply inquired, "What is all of this to you?"

The solitary man was lying on the ground, his back against the wall, clutching at his bleeding neck, and he muttered a reply in a string of barely audible words, broken up and flustered. "The flesh is everything...the taste...the look of it against the light...the muscles pushing up against it, forming such intricate designs...the beauty of it torn asunder from the body...the warmth of it in my hands...but not the blood...the blood is a fallacy...the blood ruins the spectacle of the flesh...it steals the charm of flesh...oh, but the taste of flesh...oh, the taste..."

The man spoke such insults of the blood, and to insult the blood, was to insult the vampire. He hadn't come upon such a lowly creature. Yes, he hunted humans for blood, but he tortured no one, and this heap of garbage relished in it.

The disgusting man inspired wretched ambitions in the vampire. He imagined shoving the solitary man's face into the dead husband's torso and letting him drown in guts. About to act out on that impulse, he made his way towards the man when he suddenly felt ill. He was dizzy, the ceiling like the spin cycle of a front loading washing machine. Reeling from the internal attack, he plummeted to the floor a paralyzed mess.

The solitary man recovered in that moment, his neck wound gummed up and already healed. He stood up, confident and ever so pleased with himself. Eying the felled creature on the floor, he couldn't believe his eyes. "If you're what I think you are, you're going to save me a lot of trouble, friend."

Collecting the dead husband, the man propped him back up on the hooks, jamming them between his shoulder blades this time. The corpse hung limp, dripping blood onto the floor. The solitary man stood back and watched the body, and he kept saying, "Just wait...any second...any second...you'll see it happen."

Any second turned out to be four long minutes of the corpse dripping the precious red. The vampire could hear every patter go off like a gong with his ear up against the floor. He couldn't move an inch. No sensation in his body.

Then the amazing occurred.

The dead husband's body began to shift. Quivered and trembled about its arms, torso, and legs, as if the muscles were suffering spasms. Then sliver by strand, meaty pieces sloughed off the corpse, the flesh coming undone, until all that was left was a blood stained set of bones, rough muscle tissue, and juicy organs that stayed tucked neatly in their cavities.

The solitary man collected the flesh and worked overtime to spray the blood off, and then he used clothespins to hang the flaps out on the long cord that stretched out across the room to dry. Finished with that duty, the psychopath moved to a tray of tools and selected a large pair of surgical scissors and began snipping off the vampire's clothing until he was a naked white thing on the floor.

"Any moment...it'll happen to you."

Screaming in agony, he located his voice, though his body remained useless to him, as chunks and pieces flensed themselves effortlessly from his bones, as if he'd been slow cooked, and the meat just slid off of him.

On his hands and knees, the solitary man scooped up the pieces and began spraying them clean.

He said to the vampire in jest, "I didn't realize there were other creatures of the night out there. I thought I was it. You see, I've had a craving for skin my entire life. I was born with it. Maybe genetics, but more likely it's an abnormality in the human code. My mom disowned me, but my dad kept me alive, feeding me, until he was too old to commit murder, so I was on my own, and I lived out here, feasting on hikers, or when I had to, I ventured into town for my meat. I paint it, I eat it, I relish everything about the flesh, but if what I think will happen with you does happen, you'll save me so much trouble, as I said. You'll be the solution I've been waiting for. My blood is like a narcotic. Drinking it, it allowed that woman to pose for me for hours on end. It changes the composition of the human body. My blood can enact my thoughts. Attack the body like a cancer. Paralyze it. Brainwash people to slice their own skin off in front of me. It's all a game of flesh. I record it for my entertainment, because I can't get enough."

The vampire listened, though he stopped after seeing strand by strand, layer by layer, his skin began to grow back on his body. His body was capable of miraculous feats of regeneration, and in an hour, he was intact again, though he remained motionless.

Forever crippled.

Forever at the solitary man's mercy.

The man wheeled out a cart of sharp archaic implements he'd never seen before, or could ever fathom until now. Next, the man checked the video camera in the corner to ensure it was recording. Now that everything was set in motion, the deviant gave him a craven smile and whispered to the vampire, "With you here, I'll never run out of flesh again..."

Hollywood
John Irvine

Hollywood has a lot to answer for.

I mean, look at what it did to spaghetti and westerns.

I'm a vampire. Just your average, every-day night-guy, trying to get by in an increasingly hostile environment. I don't ask for much — peace and quiet, a nice dirt-filled coffin to rest in and an occasional meal.

Not that I need to eat all that often. Well, I don't eat at all, *per se*…a liquid nightcap now and then. That's not much to ask for, surely. I mean, Hollywood has our "victims" being turned into empty cicada cases left piled tragically beside rural American roadsides! I'd love to know who thought that one up! At the very least these "victims" become blood-sucking scourges preying on hordes of penniless downtown Angelos. Ha ha…That's Hollywood.

What a joke! I give them a steak dinner at Morton's, a good Napa Valley red and intelligent conversation. I kiss their fingertips. We talk share prices and futures stocks. During a cab ride around the sights of the city afterwards, I do my thing. No vulgar plunging of canines — just a gentle scraping of the skin, and a lick or three, and we're off. No harm done. No mess. No corpse. Of course, I have to cleanse their mind of the incident. Zap! They go home none the worse for wear, half a pint of blood less, and find themselves eating liver and spinach for a week.

Hollywood is shameless.

I mean, who wears those capes anymore? They went out with Bela Lugosi, for God's sake. Can you imagine trying to flag a Yellow Cab whilst wearing a black opera cloak with a red silk lining, and dragging a limp, exsanguinated human lunchbox along the pavement?

"Taxi? Taxi? Can ve rrrride in ze cab vhile I suck ze blood from zis beautiful but trrrragic starlet who is about to die? Arrre you minding if I leave herrr in ze cab?"

Gimme a break! I don't even speak Italian, let alone Transylvanian! Sheesh. And the risks I take these days. I mean, who knows which of these bimbos is loaded? Of course I check their arms and legs and eyeballs for needle tracks—who wouldn't? But how do you tell if they're crack-heads? Or doped on amphetamines? Ecstasy? God only knows what else...by the time you've glugged your nightly half-pint, it's too late.

Hollywood stinks.

I mean, where did the bat thing come from? I hate bats. Smelly and scary. They have disgusting habits. Why on earth, (or anywhere else) would I want to flap up to a 25th floor apartment window tricked out like Batman? For one thing the smog would kill me. You can't metamorphose on the ledges for pigeon crap, and the windows up there don't even open! What the Hell are they scared of up there? Bats?

Sure, I sleep in a coffin filled with graveyard dirt. So what? If you haven't tried it, don't knock it. It sits in a nice apartment on a velvet-covered dais with views of the Hollywood Sign. The dirt is heated. I have style. I have class. Sure, I only come out at night—but then so do a zillion other Los Angeles inhabitants...why single me out just because I don't show up in bar mirrors? Every night I take the risk of being mugged, raped or solicited. Or having my black patent Reeboks stolen. OK, OK... so I'm immortal. Big deal. The muggings still give me grief for a while, and as for the rapes? *(Shudder)* I don't mind the soliciting so much, as it gives me a reliable if risky take-away menu in case I miss out on drinks uptown.

Hollywood sucks. (Pardon me.)

I mean, this immortality thing. Being immortal has its drawbacks. It means you really **do** live forever...did you ever think of that? Really? Imagine how many mothers-in-law you could accumulate in an eternity. Law suits. Paternity suits, even. What about an eternity of **The Lucy Show** reruns…think about that! Staying the same age is not all it's cracked up to be. You only get the same sort of dates.

Forget the hammer and stake stuff. More Hollywood beat-up. Silver bullets? Holy water? Sunlight? Crucifixes? I'm wetting my pants. I can't be killed. Maybe damaged a bit from time to time, but I endure. That's my thing. Enduring. Eternally. What's the big deal anyway? I don't draw welfare. I don't own guns or gas-guzzling cars. I don't even watch *Days of our Lives*.

Vampires don't kill each other, either; or humans, contrary to the popular Hollywood-generated belief. I just make an occasional red corpuscle withdrawal from one of my mobile blood banks. *"Don't come to us – we'll come to you!"* I don't even have to make deposits. How cool is that? Look at it as a sort of regular blood change, just like you do with your car oil. I care about humans; after all, they're my bank, supermarket and liquor store all in one untidy package.

Then there's the graveyard thing. I wouldn't be caught dead in one. Especially at night. Bad people go there. Sick people. Undesirable people. People who should be locked away. People I wouldn't bite if I were desperate! Not that we bite people of course, as I've said before. Just a figure of speech, really. I mean, why would I want to get the cuffs of my Calvin Klein's gooey with damp grave soil when I could be relaxing in Morton's with my dinner date? Am I mad? I don't think so. If you're disillusioned, blame Louis Mayer or Sam Goldwin. Leave me out.

Crypts…are you kidding me? No air conditioning. No room service. Hard beds. Slimy walls. Dead people. No view. Do I look stupid? And they're always in bad neighborhoods. Ever noticed that? Ever see one near Hollywood and Vine? Or on Sunset Strip? I don't think so. So why expect me to inhabit shoddy real estate?

Hey…. I'm as good as the next guy.

John Irvine

That's Hollywood...!

* * *

"Five minutes, sir."

A respectful voice infested with terminal ennui drifts through the cheap plywood door, along with the heady perfume of stale cigar smoke. With a sigh I collect myself, and as I rise I look into the big mirror, striking a dramatic pose. Well, we *can* see *ourselves.* Doesn't anybody know anything anymore? I open the door and pause for a moment in the doorway, gazing at the tarnished gold star nailed there. And at the cheap plaque it hovers over: *"Dracula's Bride — sequel 3."* Hey...it's a job already! I get five mil a picture, a small musty dressing room, and all the starlets I can drink. I get to sleep late. I'm doing OK.

Gathering my long black opera cloak with the red silk lining around me, and sliding on the Louis Vuitton polarized shades, I stride off into the light.

Heh! Heh! Heh...only in Hollywood!

Meet the Contributors

Joe Filippone is currently a fulltime actor and writer living in Hollywood California who has guest starred on many TV and webseries as well as appearing in dozens of independent films, commercials, music videos and theatrical productions. As a writer, Mr. Filippone's stories have appeared in over forty anthologies. He is also the co-editor of The Undead That Saved Christmas: Vampire Edition anthology and the author of the novels Real Boys Kiss Boys and The Christmas Cottage.

An unlucky optimist with too much to worry about.
Writing under the name **John Beck** when writing fiction, John Gledson has finally fulfilled his ambition to become an author. He has a number of horror short stories published and is currently writing and researching a travel book following his quest for the ideal sausage.
He lives with his wife and four children, trying to lead a normal life. The bug for adventure and travel manifests itself on a daily basis, leaving his family to wonder if he has just gone out for a loaf of bread, or gone to Timbuku (which he had...)

T. A. Branom is a freelance writer living and working in the breathtaking Columbia River Gorge in Washington State and has been published in print and online venues including Flashes in the Dark, Fictitious Magazine, The Molotov Cocktail, and various Static Movement anthologies. She's also a columnist for Unexplained Mysteries.
Visit her website http://www.home.earthlink.net/~branom201/.

Ken Goldman is a former teacher of English and Film Studies at Philadelphia's George Washington High School. An affiliate member of the Horror Writers Association, Ken has homes on the Main Line in Pennsylvania and at the South Jersey shore depending upon his mood and the track of the sun. His short stories appear in over 600 independent press publications in the U.S., Canada, the UK, and Australia with over thirty due for publication in 2012. His book of short stories, "You Had Me At ARRGH!! : Five Uneasy Pieces by Ken Goldman" remained an all-time top ten best seller from October 2007-March 2011 at the former Genre Mall and can now be purchased at the Sam's Dot Publishers web site. In June 2010 Damnation books (http://www.damnationbooks.com) published his novella "Desiree" in downloadable eBook; print and Kindle editions are available on

Amazon.com. Ken has received seven honorable mentions in The Year's Best Fantasy & Horror Anthologies, and he has won numerous awards, too many to mention here---but he will happily supply a list. Further information on Ken Goldman and his writing can be found at the Masters of Horror website (http://moh.spruz.com/member). Ken would be famous except for the fact nobody seems to know who he is.

Aline S. Iniestra - I love writing poetry while listening to music. My writing started as a way to let personal things out; writing romantic, painful, fantastic, and ironic poems. Now I have settled to a dark, twisted, horror kind of writing. (Sometimes I roam around fantasy too.) Music and life is what inspires my work, taking from each one of them their own essences and letting them wrap my mind. Without music, I couldn't be. I consider my poetry as a way to see the beauty in that which most would consider horrible and grotesque, such as pain, loneliness, longing, death, distortion, fantasy and all those monsters (fantastic and real ones) that we all must encounter at one point of our lives. I write in English although my mother tongue is Spanish. I am a Mexican woman who works as a teacher and spends her free time reading, listening to music, writing, looking for amazing dark-fantasy-gothic art, and doing things concerning horror and gothic things…
I have 15 poems published in the poetry collection "In Darkness We Play" by Triskaideka Books. One poem in the anthology "DEADication" by Panic Press. A poem in "U-Magazine" Issue 2. One poem in the first Issue of "House of Horror Magazine", and poems, rambling and other crazy stuff on my blog http://indarknessiplay.blogspot.com/

Nate D. Burleigh hales from Vancouver Washington. When he's not working as a Long Term Disability Analyst, he's busy being a father and husband. Since becoming a father, the conglomerated stories in his mind have come to fruition in the form of bedtime stories, but the inner horror writer in him reared its ugly head and he feels he has found his story telling niche. You can follow his work at his blog http://natedburleigh.blogspot.com/ or on Facebook. Please check out his debut novel, "Sustenance" which will be published by Rainstorm Press early in March 2012.

Christopher Hiver - I live in Pennsylvania, usually write while listening to music and enjoy an occasional cigar outside on a star-filled night. I have work upcoming in Blood Moon Rising, Night to Dawn and the Winter Chills anthology. A book of short stories, "The Spaces between Your Screams" was published in 2008. Details on all my writing can be found at
www.chrishivner.com

David Bernstein is a member of the HWA, and is the author of over 50 published short stories. Some of his work appears, or will be appearing in, Best New Werewolf Tales from Books of the Dead Press, Big Foot Among Us from Coscom Entertainment and, Don't Blink from Cruentus Libri Press. He is currently working on his fourth novel, with the first three being looked at by publishers. He lives in the NYC, and hates car horns. Visit him at davidbernsteinauthor.blogspot.com and email him dbern77@hotmail.com

Ryan Neil Falcone serves an editor for Dark Moon Books and Dark Moon Digest, and is an active member of Cornell University's Irving Literary Society. His short stories have been featured in horror-themed markets such as The Absent Willow Review, Macabre Cadaver, Dark Gothic Resurrected Magazine, and Deadman's Tome, as well as numerous commercially available print anthologies. His platform of work is summarized at: www.ryanneilfalcone.com

Lori R. Lopez is a diverse author whose genres range from Horror to Fantasy and Science Fiction, along with Poetry and Nonfiction. Her titles include OUT-OF-MIND EXPERIENCES: Thirteen Tales; DANCE OF THE CHUPACABRAS (Tome One of The Tome Trilogy Of Trilogies), a Horror-Fantasy novel; POETIC REFLECTIONS: KEEP THE HEART OF A CHILD, a volume of verse, song lyrics and prose based around her offbeat "Poetic Reflections" column; CHOCOLATE-COVERED EYES, an E-book Horror sampler of six stories and a poem; and AN ILL WIND BLOWS, an amusing Horror-Fantasy novel. Her stories and poems also appear in anthologies and magazines such as "Masters Of Horror: Damned If You Don't" (Triskaideka Books), "I Believe In Werewolves" (Netbound Publishing), "Shivers -- Tingling Tales Of Terror In Tribute To The Master! H.P. Lovecraft" (Arcanum Axiom), "ePocalypse" (Pill Hill Press), "Thirsty Are The Damned" (Rainstorm Press), and "Ghosts And Haunts" (Arcanum Axiom). Fifteen of Lori's poems were published for an anthology titled "In Darkness We Play" (Triskaideka Books). Lori designs most of her book covers and unapologetically takes pride in bending the rules of writing to her style. Her website is: www.trilllogicinnoventions.com.

Jason Hughes grew up in Texas. He has been a lifelong fan of the Horror genre for thirty-five years and counting. He likes to keep his writing on a level of realism with everyday people that are placed in horrific situations. He graduated The Tom Savini's Special Effects Make-Up Program in 2004 and still does Special Effects today. Jason is the Editor of the anthology Moral Horror. He is a contributing Writer for The Houston Examiner, Beyond the

Dark Horizon, Scream TV and Writer/ Reviewer for Horrornews.net. His writings can be found in such anthologies as Nocturnal Illumination, Ladies and Gentlemen of Horror 2010, Quakes & Storms & Thadd Presley Presents Horror along with Twisted Dreams Magazine and House of Horror Magazine among others. He is also a multi-published (and transferred to audio) Poet. Jason was chosen as one of the top ten best Horror Authors of 2009-2011. He has written screenplays for Mudd Miller Films/ Rebellious Cinema, Sick Flick Productions & American – International Pictures (released The Amityville Horror and much more) as well as contributing to Dimension Films for an upcoming release. His work has been picked up by Dimension Films for consideration of screen adaptation. He is also a Drummer, t-shirt Printer, Sky Diver and avid Supporter of The West Memphis Three (www.wm3.org).

Robert Read -- Originally from south of England, the writer now resides in the Cote d'Or of Burgundy, France, with a small army of feral cats. A boarding school education, during the mid-1960s, spawned an ambition to become a writer of science fiction and horror stories; however, responsibility to a wife and son, and a career in electronic design subverted the dream until divorce in 2003 when the creative urge was re-ignited. A writer of short stories and novels, he adheres to no particular genre, although much of his writing depicts elements of the occult and paranormal.

John Irvine was born in Lower Hutt, New Zealand in 1940, but travelled widely in Australia and Papua New Guinea thereafter for 29 years. John lives with his writer/poet wife in Colville on New Zealand's picturesque Coromandel Peninsula and occasionally lets his dark side out to play with terrified local sheep. His website can be seen at: www.cooldragon.co.nz where you may find links to his various publications.
Favorite band:
Pink Floyd

Nathan Robinson lives in Scunthorpe, England with his patient wife/editor and adoring one year old twin boys. So far he's had seven stories win the www.spinetinglers.co.uk monthly competition, and six soon to be published by Static Movement. His Mexican gangster tale 'Top of the Heap' was adapted into a podcast bywww.pseudopod.org to rave reviews. Currently he is working on four anthologies of his own short stories and novellas, entitled 'Devil Let Me Go', 'The Tell of Strangers', 'Borrowed Flesh' and 'Don't Go In!'. Follow his work at www.facebook.com/NathanRobinsonWrites

Born and raised in the hood of Portland, Oregon, over the years, **Rob M. Miller** has been victimized by violent bad guys, has victimized violent bad guys, been a U.S. Army Infantryman, taught martial arts, worked security, video store clerked, washed windows, retreaded tires, and stocked products in a grocery store.

After two years of freelance stringer work for a military newspaper, he tired of nonfiction and decided to use his love of the dark, his personal terrors and talent with words, to do something more beneficial for his fellow man: Scare the hell out of him.

Rob's continuing his quest to write tales of dark woe in the Pacific Northwest, from where he moderates an online writing group (www.writers-in-action.spruz.com). His work can be found archived at The Harrow (www.theharrow.com), as well as in various American and U.K. anthologies.

Richard H. Fay currently resides in upstate New York with his wife, daughter, two cats, and a rather confused shepherd-chow mix. Formerly a laboratory technician-turned-home educator, Richard now spends his days juggling a number of writing and art projects. History, myth, folklore, legend, true tales of the supernatural, and the various speculative genres, all serve as inspiration for his creative endeavors. Many of the fruits of his labor have appeared in a variety of e-zines, print magazines, and anthologies.

Armand Rosamilia is a New Jersey boy currently living in sunny Florida, where he writes about zombies, watches the Boston Red Sox and listens to Heavy Metal music. He's still trying to figure out how to combine the three. He loves people who e-mail him and check out his works at http://armandrosamilia.wordpress.com

Alan Spencer is a horror author from Kansas City. His novels include "The Body Cartel," "Inside the Perimeter: Scavengers of the Dead," "Ashes in Her Eyes," "Zombies and Power Tools," and "Cider Mill Vampires." Each book ranges from extreme horror to creepy and atmospheric, and if you ask the author, he'll tell you nothing is held back in any case. Look him up him on Facebook or e-mail him at alanspencer26@hotmail.com

About the Editors

Charlotte Emma Gledson currently resides in the south-coastal town of Gosport, UK. Her heart however yearns to return to her roots in the Northwest of England, specifically Cumbria. With over 30 stories and poems published in anthologies and magazines, including, 'The Serial Killer Magazine', Charlotte is also penning a supernatural novel entitled, 'Bluebells for my Baby'. Her collection of unsettling stories, 'The Lonely Tree and Other Twisted Tales of Torment' is available at all good book retailers. Recently Charlotte has been posted as poetry editor for Dopamalovi Books.

Married with four gregarious children and a collection of ventriloquist dummies and porcelain dolls, she finds time relaxing while sipping wine, singing Karaoke, and going on paranormal investigations. Contact her at charlotte@gledson.co.uk www.charlottemmagledson.com

Lyle Perez-Tinics is the creator of www.UndeadintheHead.com a website dedicated to zombie books and the authors. He is the owner and Editor-in-Chief of Rainstorm Press (www.RainstormPress.com) and The Mad Formatter (www.TheMadFormatter.com) a book interior design business. He has stories in many anthologies and is currently working on two novels, *Existing Dead* and *Rising from the Tempest*. He is the mastermind behind *The Undead That Saved Christmas* charity anthology series. He also writes middle grade chapter books under his pen name, Benny Alano. www.BennyAlano.com
Twitter - @LylePerez @RainstormPress @UndeadintheHead
www.Facebook.com/RainstormPress
www.Facebook.com/UndeadintheHead

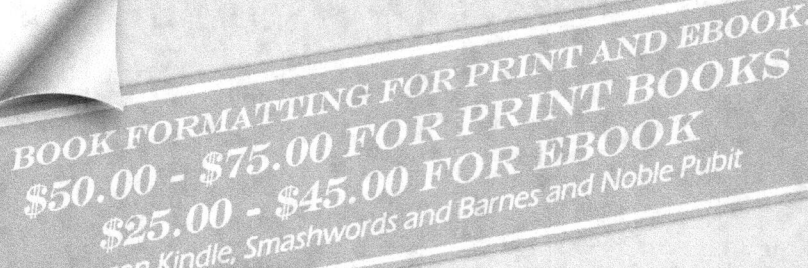

Darkness of Night

a new novel by
Mandy Tinics

Kaylee's New Year's resolution is to not take life so seriously. As a writer of paranormal romance, she leads a simple and uneventful life. She isn't searching for anything; men are the last thing on her mind. That changes when she locks eyes with a ridiculously handsome stranger. In seconds, her world is turned upside down. Sparks fly, but as quickly as the man approached, he was gone. Kaylee wonders if she will ever see him again. She can't understand how anyone could walk away from something so overwhelming.

Alec, a 253-year-old vampire, has spent years not caring about anyone. His loyalty was to his best friend, Lucian, who was more like a brother than a friend. Darkness of Night is the most popular club in the world. Alec has spent many nights watching humans and even indulges with a few, but he was not ready for what fate had in store for him.

Being half vampire and half human has made life challenging for Alec. He was raised by his human mother, and knew very little about his father. Alec knew he was different because his mother sheltered him from the world. When he looked to be in his early twenties, he finally understood why he was so different.

It is forbidden for humans to know the secret of vampire existence. Now, Alec must choose between losing his true love or jeopardizing Kaylee's life and his existence. In the end will true love conquer all or is it just a line in a book?

DARKNESS OF NIGHT
by Mandy Tinics

ISBN/EAN13: 145637768X / 9781456377687
www.CreateSpace.com/3507065

also available at Smashwords.com!

Darkness of Night is the debut novel of Mandy Tinics. She is also owner of the vampire book review site, BITE ME at www.Vampires-Bite.com

www.ingramcontent.com/pod-product-compliance
Lightning Source LLC
Chambersburg PA
CBHW070004260626
47159CB00005B/1661